Runaway!

Ashleigh felt a building sense of satisfaction as she cantered Fleet Goddess down the backstretch. The filly was moving beautifully, and Ashleigh was sure she'd made the right decision in buying her.

But then a horse suddenly galloped past close on their inside, catching Fleet Goddess by surprise. She seemed to shudder for a moment; then she thrust her head forward against the bit, yanking the reins through Ashleigh's fingers. She gave a frightened whinny and broke into a gallop.

Then, before Ashleigh knew what was happening, Fleet Goddess veered out across the track—straight toward the outside rail!

Ashleigh hauled hard on her left rein, desperately trying to change the filly's headlong course. But the filly's legs churned beneath her as she fought Ashleigh's hold.

Fighting back her panic as she saw the rail rushing toward them, Ashleigh tried to steady herself in the saddle, lifting off slightly to encourage Fleet Goddess to jump. A stride away from the rail, she squeezed hard with both legs and slid her hands forward, giving Fleet Goddess rein. The filly continued forward at the same mad pace, and Ashleigh's heart lurched. . . .

Collect all the books in the
THOROUGHBRED series:

COMING SOON
ASHLEIGH #1:
Lightning's Last Hope

THOROUGHBRED Super Editions:

Ashleigh's Christmas Miracle
Ashleigh's Diary
Ashleigh's Hope
Samantha's Journey

THOROUGHBRED

ASHLEIGH'S DREAM

JOANNA CAMPBELL

HarperPaperbacks

A Division of HarperCollins*Publishers*

This is a work of fiction. The characters, incidents, and dialogues are products of the author's imagination and are not to be construed as real. Any resemblance to actual events or persons, living or dead, is entirely coincidental.

HarperPaperbacks *A Division of* HarperCollins*Publishers*
10 East 53rd Street, New York, N.Y. 10022

Copyright © 1993 by Daniel Weiss Associates, Inc. and Joanna Campbell
Cover art copyright © 1993 Daniel Weiss Associates, Inc.

Produced by Daniel Weiss Associates, Inc., 33 West 17th Street, New York, New York 10011.

First printing: February, 1993

Printed in the United States of America

HarperPaperbacks and colophon are trademarks of HarperCollins*Publishers*

20 19 18 17 16

1

WHITE FENCE RAILS FLASHED BY AS ASHLEIGH GRIFFEN steered up the drive of Townsend Acres. All day long at school, she couldn't stop thinking about her mare, Wonder. The chestnut champion Thoroughbred was due to have her first foal at any time.

Ashleigh braked to a stop in front of her parents' house, slid out of the car, and headed directly across the graveled drive to the foaling barn. The rolling pastures of the huge Kentucky breeding and training farm stretched out around her. The grass was a brilliant fresh green, the trees were bursting forth with new leaves, and the air had the soft, sweet scent of April.

Ashleigh hurried around the corner inside the foaling barn and nearly collided with her mother. "I heard your car," Mrs. Griffen said excitedly, pushing a strand of her shoulder-length blond hair from her eyes. "Wonder's having her foal!"

"She is? Oh, my gosh! How is she?"

"Don't worry; your father and I have been with her the whole time. So far, so good."

Ashleigh rushed ahead into the dimmer light of the barn and ran down the wide, immaculately clean aisle. Her heart was pounding with excitement and fear. Wonder had nearly died at her own birth, and Ashleigh was so afraid the same thing would happen to her foal.

Ashleigh saw her father, the barn manager, Bill Parks, and several of the stable hands standing outside Wonder's stall. They turned when they saw her approaching. Her father motioned to her.

"It's going well," he said softly.

Ashleigh looked in over the stall door and saw Wonder stretched out on the thick bedding of the roomy box stall. The mare lifted her head when she saw Ashleigh and whickered softly.

"Yes, girl, I'm here!" Ashleigh whispered. "I'm so glad you waited till I got home from school to have your foal." Ashleigh turned to her father. "Can I go in?"

"I don't see why not if you're careful. She might be a little nervous and confused, especially since this is her first birth, but she trusts you."

Ashleigh quietly let herself into the stall and knelt by Wonder's head. Gently she stroked the mare's silky neck and velvet nose. "That's my girl. You're doing great," Ashleigh soothed. "Pretty soon you're going to be a mother." Wonder whuffed softly into Ashleigh's hand. Then Ashleigh felt the

2

mare's muscles stiffen as a contraction gripped her swollen belly. Ashleigh swallowed hard and looked up at her father nervously.

"She's doing fine," he reassured her.

But Ashleigh's stomach tightened as Wonder gave a low, distressed grunt. Ashleigh continued rubbing one hand gently down Wonder's neck as Wonder's soft breaths quickened. "I wish I could help you, girl," Ashleigh murmured.

When the contractions started coming more rapidly, Mr. Griffen slowly entered the stall and stood at the far side, ready if Wonder needed assistance. "It won't be much longer," he said quietly.

Suddenly Wonder lifted her head from the bedding and craned it around, grunting loudly in pain. Ashleigh could hardly keep from groaning herself as she watched her beloved horse suffer. "Oh, girl," she whispered. "I know it's scary, but you're going to be all right, and I'm here." Ashleigh's father looked over at her and spoke with subdued excitement. "The forelegs are showing. Another few contractions, and the worst will be over."

Ashleigh chewed on her lip and cradled Wonder's head as the mare struggled through several more contractions. Ashleigh had witnessed the births of many other foals, but this was Wonder, the horse she'd raised. Ashleigh felt Wonder's pain as if it were her own. *Please let everything be all right,* she prayed silently. Wonder's muscles tensed under Ashleigh's hand, and the beautiful mare strained once again. In the next moment Ashleigh saw the extended forelegs and head of the emerging foal, still covered by the white membrane of the birth sack.

Ashleigh gasped. "Your foal, girl! It's almost over now." She felt her throat closing with emotion. Wonder's copper coat had darkened with sweat, and she strained once more. Then Ashleigh gasped again in awe as the newborn's shoulders slipped free and the white membrane broke, showing a portion of a tiny, wet copper head and two delicate forelegs.

"Oh, Wonder!" Ashleigh cried. "I think your baby's going to look like you!"

Wonder seemed to sense that her ordeal was almost over. She whickered and craned her neck around as a final contraction brought her foal fully into the world. The small, sodden bundle lay curled in the straw. Within moments it was thrusting its head up as it drew the first breaths of air into its lungs. The membrane had pulled away to reveal a miniature duplicate of Wonder!

Ashleigh let out a cry of joy and hugged Wonder's neck, leaning down to kiss the mare's forehead. Wonder was looking back at her newborn, too, and suddenly gave a soft whinny of delight. The little foal's ears pricked, then it began struggling to free itself from the rest of the membrane and curl its long, delicate legs beneath it.

"It's a colt," Mr. Griffen said.

Ashleigh had trouble seeing through the mist of happy tears in her eyes. *Wonder has a son!* she thought in amazement. As long as the foal was born healthy, she hadn't cared if it turned out to be a colt or a filly. She heard the excited murmurs of those standing outside the stall. "A beauty," Bill Parks said. "Fine little fella."

Ashleigh knew not to touch the foal until Wonder had nuzzled and licked the newborn clean. Soon the mare drew her legs beneath her and reached around to proudly touch her nose to her son's. She made soft, crooning noises as she began licking the foal dry. It was such an intimate and important moment for mare and foal that Ashleigh rose and stepped back to give them their privacy.

Mr. Griffen was casting a proud and watchful eye over them, too. He glanced over at Ashleigh. "So, what do you think?"

"He's wonderful!" she said, beaming.

Soon Wonder had recovered enough strength to carefully rise to her feet. She lowered her elegant head and continued to lick her foal dry. The colt's oversize ears flicked back and forth with interest as he took in his first views of life. Within fifteen minutes, he was struggling to rise to his feet.

"He's not wasting any time, is he?" Mr. Griffen chuckled. "Just look at him."

Ashleigh couldn't take her eyes off the colt. She laughed as the tiny horse pushed awkwardly to his feet, swaying and pitching drunkenly, then falling in a tangle of legs on the soft straw, only to pick himself up and try again. Wonder whickered her encouragement, and finally the little copper foal had his legs steady enough beneath him to take a few uncertain steps to his mother's side.

"He's trying to nurse already," Ashleigh said with relief. She remembered Wonder's first hours of life, when the filly had been so weak she'd had to be helped to her mother's side.

"I don't think we're going to have to worry about any problems here," Mr. Griffen said.

Wonder turned to look at her new offspring. She whickered quietly to him, then lowered her head again to touch him gently with her nose. Ashleigh stepped to Wonder's side. "He's so beautiful, girl. I'm so proud of you!"

In answer Wonder nuzzled Ashleigh's dark hair and let out a satisfied, grunting sigh.

"I've been so worried," Ashleigh confessed. "I was afraid something might go wrong, like when you were born. But your baby's fine. He's going to grow up to be a great racehorse like you were!"

Wonder whinnied, and Ashleigh turned to see the foal suckling hungrily—and noisily. She laughed. "Aren't you something!" She reached out and gently ran a hand over his short back. "I know you're going to be special," she said.

"So, it's a little fella," said a gruff voice from outside the stall. Charlie Burke had joined the gathering there. The old, gray-haired trainer looked as disheveled as ever as he pushed back his floppy felt hat and squinted his blue eyes to study the new arrival. Charlie nodded briskly. "Nice-looking foal." That was high praise coming from Charlie, who wasn't free with compliments.

"Wonder's doing well, too." Ashleigh grinned.

"Thought she would. She's sure had plenty of nursemaids," he said, looking pleased in spite of himself.

Ashleigh heard footsteps rapidly approaching, then her twelve-year-old brother, Rory, suddenly appeared at the stall door. "Wow! The foal looks just like Wonder! Good going, girl." Wonder accepted the praise with a bob of her head.

Then the farm's owner, Clay Townsend, arrived. News always traveled fast around the farm, and Mr. Townsend had a special interest in Wonder. Though he'd turned over half ownership of Wonder to Ashleigh after Wonder had won the Breeder's Cup Classic, Wonder was still the farm's prize mare.

The year before, the filly's four-year-old season had started with a bang, with Wonder winning her first two big races—the Donn Handicap and the Santa Anita Handicap. But then Wonder had stumbled during a workout and fractured the cannon bone in her right foreleg. It was only a hairline fracture, but the injury was enough to end Wonder's racing career. Ashleigh had been devastated, but she knew the horse's injury could have been much worse. At least Wonder would eventually mend. A few weeks later, at Clay Townsend's urging, Wonder had been bred to one of the top stallions standing at stud in Kentucky.

Clay Townsend was beaming now as he looked over the stall door at mother and foal. "That's what

I like to see! A strong, healthy foal. He's definitely got Wonder's look, though I think he may have the bigger build of his sire. We just may have the next Townsend Acres champion here!"

Charlie shook his head. "Little fella's going to have a lot to live up to. He's less than an hour old and already we're expecting him to be a star."

"Look who's talking. You've probably got his training schedule already planned," Ashleigh teased.

"Not me."

"Right, Charlie," Mr. Townsend said, chuckling. He turned to the Griffens to get the details of the birth. "She had no problems at all?"

"Not one. She didn't even need us," Mr. Griffen said. "I'll have the vet look them over, of course, but I'd say they'll both get a clean bill of health. Unfortunately, it doesn't look good for one of the other mares that foaled this morning—one of the mares Townsend Pride covered. The foal's underweight and not responding well. One of the grooms is keeping an eye on them."

Mr. Townsend frowned. "Let's go have a look."

Townsend Pride was the top stallion on the farm and was Wonder's sire as well. To lose a foal he'd sired would be a huge disappointment. But at the moment, Ashleigh was too filled up with joy over Wonder's safe delivery and her beautiful son to worry too much about the weaker foal.

Wonder's colt had finished nursing, and now he was awkwardly thrusting his tiny head forward and nuzzling Ashleigh's hand. Her heart melted completely. She carefully knelt and gave the foal a gentle hug. "I suppose I ought to let you get some rest, little guy," she said softly.

"They both need to rest," Mrs. Griffen said.

Ashleigh stood and dropped a kiss on Wonder's soft nose. "I'm so proud of you, girl! You take a snooze—you deserve it—and I'll see you in a little while."

Wonder whickered, and her foal watched curiously as Ashleigh let herself out of the stall.

"You coming up to the training stables later?" Charlie asked Ashleigh.

"As soon as I call Mike and Linda and tell them the news!"

Charlie nodded and strode off.

Mrs. Griffen put her arm around Ashleigh's shoulders and gave her a squeeze. "Happy?"

"I couldn't be happier, Mom. And I'm so relieved everything went well."

"We're all happy. Come on, Rory," Mrs. Griffen added. "I need your help with a few things before you go in to do your homework."

Rory made a face, but followed behind his mother. Ashleigh hurried into her parents' office at the end of the barn. The Griffens were the breeding managers at Townsend Acres and oversaw all the mares and their young foals.

Ashleigh grabbed the phone on the cluttered desktop and quickly dialed Mike Reese's number. She had been dating Mike for almost two years, and as far as Ashleigh was concerned, they had a perfect relationship. Both of them loved Thorough-breds, racing, and training horses, and they planned on making their careers in the racing business. Mike was finishing his first year of college at the University of Kentucky in Lexington. He commuted to classes daily from his and his father's training farm, Whitebrook, on the other side of Lexington. His schedule usually left him plenty of time to supervise his training operation and see Ashleigh several times a week.

Mike picked up on the second ring.

"Hi!" Ashleigh cried when she heard his voice. "Wonder had her foal! It's a colt. They're both doing really well, and he looks just like Wonder!"

"That's great," he said. Ashleigh could hear the relief in his voice. He'd known she'd been worried. "I'll be right over. Give me ten minutes."

"See you then." Ashleigh next dialed Linda March, her best friend. "It's a boy!"

"All right!" Linda said. "Does he look like Wonder? Is she okay? Did she have any problems?"

"He looks just like her—just like she did when she was a foal, only bigger. He's fine, she's fine. Everything went perfectly."

"I was kind of hoping for a filly—you know, another Wonder—but if he's healthy, that's all that matters."

"He's just gorgeous, Linda. I can't wait till you see him."

"I'll be there in a minute," Linda said quickly. "I can't stay long because I have tennis practice at school, but I'll be there." Linda was an incredible tennis player and a talented horsewoman, and now that the two girls were in their junior year at Henry Clay High, Linda was co-captain of the school tennis team.

After she'd hung up the phone, Ashleigh quietly slipped down the barn aisle to take one last look at Wonder and the foal. They were both resting peacefully on the thick bedding. She hated to leave them, but she knew they needed their rest.

Once outside, Ashleigh crossed the graveled drive to her family's house and hurried up to the bedroom to change into her work jeans. When her super-neat older sister, Caroline, was home from college, Ashleigh never dared spread her mess over the invisible line that divided the room in half. But now, the place looked very lived in, with magazines and books piled on every surface, riding gear stuck in every corner, and clothes discarded on both beds.

Ashleigh was coming down the front porch steps when Mike's battered but serviceable pickup came up the long drive. He parked in front of the house, climbed out, and gave Ashleigh a big hug. His thick blond hair was tousled and his blue eyes were sparkling. Ashleigh looked up at him with a grin. "They're resting, but we can sneak in for a quick look."

Mike laughed. "Not excited or anything, are you?" he teased.

Ashleigh giggled. "Listen," she said defensively,

11

"even Charlie was acting like an old softy, and Mr. Townsend was grinning from ear to ear."

As they headed toward the barn, Linda arrived in her mother's station wagon. She hurried over, smiling, her blond curls in their usual disarray. "Come on. What are you waiting for? Let's go," she said.

The three of them went into the barn and stood looking over Wonder's stall door for several minutes. The foal was curled in a furry copper ball, sound asleep. Wonder drowsily blew out a soft breath of greeting, then dozed off again.

"You're right," Linda whispered. "He looks just like her. I can't believe it. It's funny to think of Wonder being a mother. I mean, it hardly seems like any time at all since she was just a foal."

"I know." Ashleigh sighed. "A lot sure has happened since then."

"What are you going to call him?" Mike asked, keeping his voice down.

"Well, Mr. Townsend said that I could name him, so I've given it a lot of thought. What do you guys think of Wonder's Pride?"

"That's perfect, Ashleigh," Mike said with approval.

"Yeah," Linda agreed.

"Okay. Wonder's Pride it is, then."

They stood gazing into the stall a few minutes longer, then Linda checked her watch. "I've got to go or I'll be late for practice." She reached out and gave Ashleigh a quick hug. "Congratulations, buddy. I'll see you in the morning. See you later, Mike," she added in a cheery whisper before hurrying outside.

"We'd better go, too," Ashleigh said to Mike. "Charlie's waiting to see us up at the training stables."

Mike took Ashleigh's hand as they started up the drive. "I'll be glad when I get my own breeding operation together," he said.

"Well, you already have your first stallion."

"But no mares," Mike added with a laugh.

"Just wait until Jazzman wins the American Championship Racing Series," Ashleigh told him confidently. "Then you'll have the money you need to really get your operation started."

"That would be nice, but we'll see."

"And look how well he's doing already." Ashleigh had a lot of confidence in both Mike and Jazzman, the black four-year-old colt Mike had trained by himself. Jazzman had missed the Triple Crown the year before because of an injury, but he was doing amazingly well this year.

"Yeah," Mike agreed. "He's been pretty fantastic, but you know how much can go wrong. I just want to take each race as it comes and not get my hopes up too high."

Ashleigh squeezed his arm. "Well, I can't help getting my hopes up. I haven't got any of my own horses to cheer on this year, so I'm counting on Jazzman. Charlie's got a couple of okay horses in training, but I know none of them is going to be another Wonder."

"Maybe you'll be able to find a good horse to

train this weekend. We're still going to the Smith Farm bankruptcy auction, aren't we?"

"Definitely," Ashleigh answered quickly. Ashleigh desperately wanted another special horse to train. After working on a champion like Wonder, it just wasn't the same riding the horses in Charlie's string. She had finally persuaded her parents to let her use part of her share of Wonder's earnings to buy one. "You know, my parents weren't too keen about letting me use Wonder's prize money," she said to Mike. "But I've got enough saved to pay for two college educations, and aside from buying my car, I haven't spent one dime of it."

"It'll be a risk, though," Mike said. "You'll be buying a horse without knowing how it will perform—or even if it will perform."

"Wouldn't *you* take a risk? I'll bet you would," Ashleigh said, challenging him.

Mike laughed. "I've already taken a couple. Yeah, I'd do the same thing you're doing."

"Besides," Ashleigh added, "I have a ten-thousand-dollar limit, and if I don't see a horse I like, I won't buy one. Charlie says the Smiths are supposed to have some good stock, though, and the prices might be cheap since it's a bankruptcy sale."

"Are you going to ask him to come?"

Ashleigh grinned. "He's just waiting for an invitation. You *know* he's looking for another Wonder, too. It'll be almost two years before Wonder's Pride can race."

CHARLIE WAS LEANING AGAINST A TREE JUST OUTSIDE one of the stable buildings when Ashleigh and Mike approached. With him were Hank, one of the oldest and most respected grooms in the stable, and Wonder's former jockey, Jilly, whose career had skyrocketed after her successes with Wonder. Jilly used to spend nearly all of her time at the farm, riding Townsend Acres horses, but now she was in demand. She traveled to major tracks on the East Coast and had more mounts than she'd ever hoped for.

Hank and Jilly greeted Ashleigh and Mike with smiles, and Charlie gave Mike a welcoming nod. The taciturn old man really seemed quite fond of Mike. Ashleigh thought he had taken to him because he respected Mike's seriousness about horses and training.

"Been to see the foal?" Charlie asked.

"I sure have," Mike answered. "He's looking great."

"He's something, all right," Hank agreed. "Definitely the best-looking foal so far this year."

"How's Jazzman coming along?" Charlie asked Mike. "You still looking at the Pimlico Special next month?"

"Yup." Mike nodded. "I gave him a couple of weeks rest, but I'll put him back in training next week and keep my fingers crossed."

"He's a good horse. You're doing a good job with him," Charlie said shortly. Mike beamed at the praise. "You hear Maddock started a new assistant trainer today?" Charlie asked Ashleigh.

"No. I didn't know he had found someone."

"Seems like a nice young guy," Hank put in. "Name's Ian McLean."

"Sad story," Charlie mused. "His wife was killed in a training accident a year ago. The young horse she was riding bolted, went through the rail, and threw her. She broke her neck in the fall."

"How awful!" Ashleigh gasped.

"He has a daughter, too," Charlie said. "Gotta be hard on the kid to have lost her mother. She's only thirteen or so. I saw her wandering around today."

As they talked, Ashleigh noticed a slim girl watching them from across the stable yard. The girl was hard to miss. A mane of brilliant red hair fell to her shoulders. "Is that his daughter over there?" Ashleigh asked.

Charlie glanced across the yard. "Yup. That's her."

"I ought to make friends with her. She must be feeling pretty lonely in a new place." Ashleigh remembered how lost she had felt when her family first arrived at Townsend Acres five years before. She had hated leaving her old home and all her friends. She began to motion for the McLean girl to come over, but the redhead was already moving off, disappearing into one of the other buildings.

Ashleigh was still watching the girl depart when Charlie spoke to her. "You still going to that dispersal auction this weekend?"

Ashleigh turned back to the old trainer. "Yeah. In fact, Mike and I were just talking about it."

Charlie scratched his gray head and absently stared into the distance. "With that farm going bankrupt, you might be able to pick up something decent."

Ashleigh winked at Mike. She kept Charlie in suspense a second longer, then said mildly, "If you have time, you could come along."

Charlie frowned. "Yup. Guess I could. Never know what you might find."

"It's Sunday afternoon," Ashleigh said. "The auction starts at one. We should get there at least an hour before to check out the horses."

"I'll be ready," Charlie said.

Ashleigh and Mike stayed at the training stables a while longer gossiping with Hank and Jilly, but then Mike had to start heading back to tend to his own horses. They walked down the curving drive together, then parted with a quick kiss at Mike's pickup.

"I'll try to stop by tomorrow," Mike said. "Otherwise, I'll call."

Ashleigh nodded and smiled as he backed up and rolled off down the drive. Then she crossed the drive to the foaling barn to check on Wonder and her foal. It was nearly dinnertime, and it was pretty quiet in the barn. Ashleigh waved to Bill Parks as she passed his office, then walked down the barn aisle toward Wonder's stall.

She was surprised to find someone already standing there. The girl's slim, boyish figure and mop of red hair were unmistakable. It was the new assistant trainer's daughter.

She had rested her arms on the stall half door and was quietly watching Wonder and Wonder's Pride. She jumped and gave a guilty start when Ashleigh said hello.

"I just wanted to see them," she said defensively. "Everyone was talking about them in the training barns."

Ashleigh smiled reassuringly. "It's okay. Wonder doesn't mind having admirers. Do you, girl?"

Wonder whickered in greeting, then stepped across the stall to nudge Ashleigh with her velvet nose. Wonder's Pride quickly wobbled after her.

"I'm Ashleigh Griffen. You must be the new trainer's daughter."

The girl nodded. "I'm Samantha McLean—but people usually call me Sammy. You sure it's okay if I'm here?" she asked a little nervously.

"It's okay with me, and since I own half of

18

Wonder and her foal, that's good enough. And you know, you can come here anytime you want. I know how hard it is to move to a new place. I had a hard time when my family first came here, but I think you'll grow to like it."

"I like it already," Samantha said softly, "though it's kind of hard not knowing anybody."

"Everyone who works here is pretty friendly. Where did you live before?" Ashleigh asked.

"All over the place. We moved around a lot, on or near different tracks—wherever my father could find a job."

"That must have been rough."

"It was," Samantha agreed. "But I think it's going to be better here. A farm is more like a home than a racetrack is." Samantha turned her bright green eyes away from Ashleigh and looked back at Wonder's Pride, who had nestled in the thick bedding of the stall. "He really is beautiful, just like his mother. You know, I heard about Wonder before I even got here—everybody's heard about Ashleigh's Wonder." She paused. "I saw you ride her in the Breeder's Cup when I was only eleven. Are you riding or training any horses now?"

"I exercise-ride for Charlie Burke. He's the older trainer who always wears a floppy hat."

"Oh, I've seen him around."

"And sometimes I ride for him in races—but only the local ones. I'm riding Silverjet in a race at Keeneland on Saturday. Do you ride?"

"I used to," Samantha said shortly. "Now I just

help my father with grooming and things."

"You must know quite a bit about training if you've always lived around racetracks."

"I guess." Samantha pursed her lips. "There's a lot more I want to learn, though. This is the first time I've been around really decent horses. My father used to train a lot of claimers. But he's a good trainer. He never had a chance to show what he could do before."

"He'll have some nice horses to work with here, and I think he'll like Mr. Maddock." Ashleigh pushed a strand of hair behind her ear and studied Samantha, whose eyes hadn't left Wonder and her foal. "Since you're interested in training, why don't you come out and watch Charlie and me work the horses in the morning?"

Samantha looked at Ashleigh, her eyes shining with excitement. But then she suddenly grew serious again. "My father told me not to get in anybody's way. This job is too important to him."

"You won't be in anyone's way," Ashleigh assured her. "I'd like you to come, and Charlie won't mind. We start early, as soon as it's light—but I guess you know that."

Samantha nodded. "I'll be there."

Ashleigh smiled. "Great! Now, do you want to go in and have a closer look at Wonder's Pride? Wonder won't mind, will you, girl?"

"Is that what his name is—Wonder's Pride?" Samantha asked as Ashleigh unlatched the stall door.

"It isn't official yet, but that's what I'm going to call him."

The foal struggled to get his spindly legs under him and greet his visitors. Samantha eagerly stepped inside.

The next morning, Samantha was already waiting at the rail of the training oval when Ashleigh made her way up the drive. The sky was lit by a misty, early-morning light, and the grass was wet with dew. Ashleigh saw that Ken Maddock, the head trainer, already had a couple of horses out working. A tall, slender man with thick auburn hair was standing with him, watching the horses on the oval. Ashleigh guessed he was Ian McLean.

She motioned for Samantha to join her at one of the stable buildings where Charlie would be checking over and tacking up the horses to be worked that morning. Birds chirped in the trees, but there was still a bite to the April morning air. Ashleigh zipped up the lightweight jacket she was wearing, though she knew she'd be feeling a lot warmer after she'd worked a few horses.

"Morning," Ashleigh said when Samantha joined her. "Charlie's in the stable. Let's go see which horse he wants me to work first."

Charlie was standing outside one of the stalls, tacking up Silverjet, a dark gray stallion. Hank held the horse as Charlie worked, and waved when he saw Ashleigh and Samantha approaching.

"Hi, Hank. Hi, Charlie," Ashleigh called.

"Yup," Charlie said brusquely as he tightened the saddle girth.

"This is Samantha McLean," Ashleigh said.

"We've already met." Hank smiled.

"I told her she could watch the workouts," Ashleigh added to Charlie.

"Fine with me," Charlie said. He nodded to Samantha, then spoke to Ashleigh. "Okay, missy, he's set. Lead him out. Hank, you can bring out Stalker in a couple of minutes."

Ashleigh took the gray's reins and started leading him out across the tree-rimmed stable yard toward the training track. Samantha walked along beside her. Ashleigh stopped a few yards from the gap onto the track and pulled down the stirrups. "Charlie usually watches from the rail to the right of the gap," Ashleigh explained to Samantha, who was looking a little uncertain. "You can stand there with him."

Charlie shuffled up and gave Ashleigh a leg into the saddle. "Give him a good half-mile breeze, then gallop him out another four furlongs. That should get him tuned up for the race. Then we'll give him another light workout on Wednesday or Thursday."

Ashleigh settled herself in the saddle, collected the reins firmly in her hands, and tapped Silverjet's sides with her heels. As the horse moved toward the track, she glanced over to see Samantha watching her intently.

Ashleigh moved Silverjet counterclockwise up the track at a walk, then a trot, along the outside rail of the mile oval. Two other horses were working at a gallop along the inside. They swept past and moved into the turn. Ashleigh kept the gray at a steady trot until they'd cleared the turn themselves, then she glanced behind her and saw that the track was clear. She moved Silverjet in and gave him the signal to canter.

Silverjet's warm breath steamed out in the cool air, and his feet pounded a steady, thudding rhythm on the harrowed dirt of the track. Ashleigh held him at a canter around the oval. As they came out of the far turn and down the stretch toward the mile marker pole, she eased Silverjet in closer to the rail. She crouched lower in the saddle over the stallion's withers, slid her hands up along his neck, giving him more rein, and shouted, "Go!"

He jumped out into a gallop, but he wasn't putting out the speed Charlie wanted. Ashleigh kneaded her hands along his neck, clucking, and the horse put his mind to it. She kept him at a brisk gallop, not letting him slack off, as they whipped around half the oval. The wind rushed at her, and her ears echoed with the sound of his pounding hooves and evenly snorted breaths. Only as they swept past the half-mile marker did she ease off and let him settle, galloping out the next four furlongs without pressure.

As they passed the mile marker pole again, Ashleigh stood in the stirrups and drew back steadily on the reins. Silverjet immediately dropped into a canter, then a trot. Ashleigh patted his neck and turned him back toward the gap. "Attaboy," she praised. "Nice job!" The horse tossed his head.

Charlie seemed satisfied as she rode off the oval toward him. He nodded as he looked the horse over. "He's come out of the work in good shape. He should be ready for Saturday, not that I'm expecting a win. Okay, take Stalker out."

Ashleigh dismounted, pulled up the stirrups, and traded Silverjet for the two-year-old bay colt Hank was holding. Stalker, she knew, would be more of a handful. He was nearing the end of his preliminary training, and Charlie was preparing him for his first race, which would probably be in late spring. He was young and full of high spirits.

"Keep him in hand," Charlie told her when she was in the saddle. "Give him an easy two-mile gallop, but don't let him push the pace. He's got to learn to mind his rider."

"We'll just take it nice and slow today, fella," Ashleigh said as she collected his reins firmly and moved toward the track.

The morning workouts weren't anywhere near as exciting as riding in a race, but Ashleigh loved every minute she was in the saddle—even the wet days when she'd come off the oval liberally coated in mud. This was where she wanted to be, working with horses, channeling and focusing their strength and bringing out the best in them.

An hour later, after Ashleigh had worked two more horses, they were finished for the morning.

Ashleigh jumped off the last horse, and Hank led it off. Ken Maddock and Ian McLean were still at the rail, watching the last of Maddock's horses work.

After Charlie had ambled off after Hank, Ashleigh turned to Samantha. "So, what did you think?"

"It's different from the track. More relaxed. You don't have all the other trainers watching every move you make, which is probably better for the horses."

"It is, I think, but these horses will need at least one work at the track so that they can get used to it. Come and watch anytime you want," Ashleigh added.

"Thanks, I will. I'd better go. There's my father waving at me. It's my first day of school, and he's taking me in to register. I'll see you later—and thanks for letting me come."

Ashleigh watched as Samantha rushed over to join her father. Then she turned and headed for her house. She still had to shower, change, and pick up Linda at her house a half-mile up the road before going to school.

Samantha showed up at the training oval the next two mornings. She watched the workouts intently and listened closely to every comment Charlie or Ashleigh made. It seemed she didn't miss a thing that went on in or around the training stables.

Linda came home with Ashleigh on Thursday afternoon, the one day she didn't have tennis practice. Ashleigh introduced her to Samantha, but

Samantha didn't stay to talk with them. "I've started helping muck out the stalls," she said, "and my dad has some tack he wants me to clean."

"Does she get paid for helping?" Linda asked as Samantha hurried off.

"I doubt it," Ashleigh answered, "but I think she enjoys doing it. She really likes being around the stables."

"Sounds like you."

Ashleigh grinned. "What's wrong with that?"

"Oh, nothing—just look where it got you."

The sound of tires spitting gravel caught the two girls' attention. A sleek Ferrari roared past them and screeched to a stop farther up the yard.

"Well, look who's back," Linda said sourly. "What's Brad doing home from college already? It's only April."

Ashleigh made a face. She and the farm owner's son, Brad Townsend, did not get along. Brad might be tall and handsome, with half the girls in Lexington drooling over him, but in Ashleigh's opinion he was a rude and arrogant spoiled brat. "He must be home for a long weekend," Ashleigh said. "I'll just have to keep out of his way."

Linda laughed. "I thought maybe now that Wonder isn't racing against his horse, he'd be less of a pain."

"Brad doesn't know how to be anything *but* a pain." Ashleigh frowned, then looked at Linda, and both of them started to giggle. "Come on. Let's go see the foal."

Ashleigh managed to steer clear of Brad that evening, but on Friday morning he was at the rail with Ken Maddock and Ian McLean, loudly voicing his own opinions about the horses in training. Twice he took a horse away from its regular exercise rider and rode it off for its workout himself.

Inside the stables, he was worse. He ordered the grooms and stable hands around until most of the staff wore angry scowls on their faces.

"He acts like he's God or something," Ashleigh muttered to Jilly. "I can't understand why his father lets him get away with it."

Jilly pulled a piece of hay from a nearby hay net and chewed on it. "Because Brad will be taking over when Mr. Townsend retires."

"Half the staff's going to end up quitting," Ashleigh said.

Jilly shrugged. "At least he's only here part of the time."

Samantha strode up the aisle, carrying an armful of dirty rags and blankets to the laundry room. She was glowering, and her green eyes were practically sending out sparks.

"What's wrong?" Ashleigh asked.

Samantha jerked her head backward. "Him!"

Ashleigh looked past Samantha and saw Brad at the other end of the barn.

"Do this . . . do that!" Samantha said, mimicking him. "I don't like him one bit. I've been around people like him before, at the track," she said, fuming. "They're always right, so there's no point in arguing. My dad says to just hear them out, then do what you were going to do in the first place. They never even notice. But I'm staying away from him!"

Charlie came into the stable and motioned to Jilly. "Maddock wants to talk to you about your races this weekend. He's in the office."

"I'm on my way." Jilly straightened up and flipped her long blond braid over her shoulder. "Don't let Brad get to you," she said softly to Samantha. "Ashleigh can tell you all about it. See you later, guys."

Ashleigh followed Samantha to the laundry room. "I'm going down to visit Wonder and the foal," she said. "Why don't you come with me and get away from here for a while?"

"Sure," Samantha said quickly. "I'm done anyway." The girl's brow was still furrowed, but as they walked down the drive to the breeding barns, Samantha seemed to cheer up a little.

"Brad will be gone by Sunday night," Ashleigh told her.

Samantha lifted her shoulders and huffed a sigh. "He just really made me angry."

"I know. Brad's made me angry, too."

"Well, next time I'll just stay out of his way." They walked a few paces in silence, then Samantha asked, "Are you nervous about the race tomorrow?"

"A little," Ashleigh answered. "I've ridden in enough races so that I'm getting used to it, but I always get a case of the jitters just before post time.

28

You should have seen me the first time I rode." Ashleigh laughed at the memory. "I was an absolute wreck. I was so sure I'd totally mess up. But I didn't. Once we were in the gate and I started concentrating, I forgot to be nervous."

"You're still an apprentice, aren't you?"

"And I will be for a long time. With school and all, I don't get to ride enough to qualify. I'm too young anyway. Jilly rode for years as an apprentice and didn't qualify for her regular license until the year Wonder started racing."

"I'd like to watch the race tomorrow."

"Well, come with me," Ashleigh said. "I'm driving over by myself an hour or so before the race starts."

Samantha jammed her hands in her jacket pockets and frowned. "I'll ask my father, but I think he'll probably want me to stay here."

"Charlie and my boyfriend, Mike, will be there, too, so you won't be left alone while I'm riding."

"That's not it, exactly." Samantha shrugged. "I'll ask him."

Ashleigh sensed that there was some sort of trouble between Samantha and her father, but she didn't know her well enough to ask her what it was. She could only hope that Samantha would be able to talk about it when they became better friends.

AS IT TURNED OUT, SAMANTHA'S FATHER SAID IT WAS okay for her to go to the races, and she and Ashleigh headed for the track in Lexington at noon on Saturday.

The Keeneland track was one of the most beautiful in the country. By the time Ashleigh and Samantha got there, the stabling area was alive with activity. The air echoed with the calls of horses as grooms led sleek Thoroughbreds around the yard. Some horses were being bathed in the dappled sunlight, and others were being prepared for their journey to the track.

"This way," Ashleigh said as the two girls walked toward the barns. "Charlie should be a couple of barns down in the Townsends' regular stabling area." She glanced over at Samantha and saw the excitement on the younger girl's face.

"This is my first time at the track since—"

Samantha hesitated. "Well, it's been a long time."

"We'll have fun today," Ashleigh said, hoping there wouldn't be any mishaps on the track to remind Samantha of her mother's accident.

Silverjet was entered in a small allowance race. Neither Ashleigh nor Charlie had any huge expectations that he'd win, but as always, Ashleigh would give it her best. She waved when she saw Charlie standing outside Silverjet's stall.

"I was about to take him to the receiving barn," Charlie said as they walked up. "Jilly's down at the end of the stable talking to Maddock. And Mike just went to check on Indigo, but he'll be back."

"So he *did* make it," Ashleigh said, smiling. "He was afraid he'd be held up in town and miss the race."

"Maybe he'll bring us luck," Charlie muttered as he led Silverjet, groomed and sheeted, from his stall. "We'll need it."

The old trainer was getting bored and grumpy again. Ashleigh knew he was disappointed with the horses he was training that year. It was hard for him to work with mediocre runners after he'd trained Wonder to championship status. She only hoped a new star would show up in Charlie's two-year-old crop, and maybe she'd be able to find a good horse at the following day's auction. If she did, she'd need Charlie's advice and help with its training.

She heard Mike's familiar voice call from behind her. "Here you are!" He put an arm around her shoulders and gave her a squeeze.

"Mike, this is Samantha McLean," Ashleigh said, "the new assistant trainer's daughter. Sammy, Mike Reese."

"Hi, Sammy," Mike said, giving the girl a friendly smile.

Samantha smiled shyly in return.

Ashleigh turned to Mike. "How's Indigo?" she asked.

"He'll be ready for next week's race, if nothing goes wrong, and I think he'll do better than he did at his last race."

"I know he will," Ashleigh said. Indigo was another four-year-old Mike had trained, but while Jazzman had already racked up victories, Indigo was only just starting to come into his own and improve. "You've got him right where he should be."

A moment later Jilly strode toward them, smiling from ear to ear.

"Maddock must have had some good news for you," Mike said to her.

"It has nothing to do with Maddock. Craig just called. He'll be here tomorrow!"

"All right!" Ashleigh laughed. "I guess we won't be seeing much of you then."

Jilly grinned. "You're right about that!" Jilly had been dating Craig Avery, one of the top jockeys in the country, for the last two years. Since they both had heavy riding schedules at different tracks, they didn't have a lot of free time to spend together. But when they were together, they were inseparable.

"You're riding in the third race, too, aren't you?" Ashleigh asked Jilly.

"Yeah, for one of the other trainers. Though now it's not going to be easy to keep my mind on business," Jilly said with a laugh.

"Don't worry. You won't be thinking about anything but the race once you get out on the track," Mike told her.

"That's true. And I'm only riding in three races this afternoon, so it shouldn't be too bad." She turned to Ashleigh. "We should probably head up to the jockeys' room and get changed."

Ashleigh nodded and looked at Samantha. "You can hang out with Mike while we get ready. We'll see you guys at the walking ring."

"Come on, Sammy. I'll show you Indigo," Mike offered.

Samantha smiled. "Okay. I'd really like that."

"Sammy seems like a nice kid," Jilly said as she and Ashleigh headed toward the jockeys' quarters.

"Yeah," Ashleigh said tentatively, "but I get the feeling that something's making her unhappy."

"It wouldn't be surprising after her mother's accident."

"Mmmm, but I think it's even more than that."

Thirty minutes later Ashleigh and Jilly were in the walking ring, ready to mount up. Mike and Samantha stood a few yards away.

"Ride the race like we planned," Charlie told Ashleigh as he gave her a leg into the saddle. "Get him right out on the lead and keep him there. There's no other speed horse in the race, though you're going to have to watch for some late closers. Nurse him along and keep the pace moderate, and just hope his tank doesn't run dry before the wire."

"Will do," Ashleigh said as she settled in the short-stirruped racing saddle and picked up the reins. She wore the green-and-gold silks of Townsend Acres. Across the ring she saw Jilly in the silks of another stable, mounted on a dark bay.

The horses and riders started moving out of the walking ring. Ashleigh patted Silverjet's sleek gray neck. "Okay, boy, let's go out there and do our best."

The stallion huffed and pricked his ears as they walked forward. Ashleigh felt a small bubble of nervousness in her stomach. It wasn't a big race, but even the least important races could be filled with excitement and danger. Besides, she really wanted to win this one for Charlie. She took a deep breath, straightened her shoulders, and put her mind on business.

The viewing stands were completely full, but Silverjet was used to the noise. He was calm during the post parade and warm-up jog, and he loaded smoothly into the gate. They were in post position four in the eight-horse field. Since they were right in the middle of the pack, Ashleigh knew she would have to break Silverjet fast and get him out of the crush and right to the front.

Ashleigh adjusted herself in the saddle, gathered up the reins, and wrapped her fingers in the horse's mane to steady her seat as they came out of the gate. She carried a whip, though Charlie hated to see it used on any of his horses unless absolutely necessary. She tucked it under her arm, then waited alertly with her head up and eyes focused between Silverjet's ears. A second later, the bell sounded and the gate doors flew open. Ashleigh heeled Silverjet and shouted, "Go!"

He jumped out from the gate, thrusting with his powerful hindquarters. Seven horses to either side of them jumped out at the same time. Ashleigh kneaded her hands along Silverjet's neck, asking him for speed, and he responded, bringing them to the front. Gradually as they swept away from the gate she moved him in, close to the inside rail, then let him settle in a steady, ground-eating gallop. She glanced quickly under her arm behind them and saw that they had a length lead on the next horse in the field. If she could keep the pace easy, Silverjet might have enough left to keep off the rest of the field at the wire—but there was a chance he would tire and fall behind.

The race was a mile long, and as they swept down the backstretch, Ashleigh looked ahead around the far turn, calculating when to ask Silverjet to accelerate. She couldn't ask him too soon, or he'd be used up before the finish. *Patience*, she told herself, *patience*.

As they went into the turn, she glanced back again. She saw several horses gaining on them and fought the instinct to push Silverjet for more speed too soon. *Easy, easy,* she told herself.

Then they were into the stretch. She saw the wire ahead. "Now!" she cried to the horse. Again she kneaded her hands along Silverjet's neck, giving him all the rein he needed. He put everything he had into it, lengthening his stride. They stayed a steady length in front of the rest of the field, but Ashleigh knew the horse would be used up soon.

She could hear the hoofbeats and snorted breaths of the horse coming up on their outside. She flicked the crop along the side of the stallion's head—not touching him, just letting him see it. "Just a little more, Silver!" she cried. "Come on, boy, just a little more!"

The horse responded. She felt him give one last surge. They were under the wire. And they were still in front! A horse shot past them on the outside, but it didn't matter anymore. They'd won!

She stood in the stirrups and pulled him back to a canter. "Good boy!" she said, patting him proudly on the neck. "You gave it everything you had. Charlie's going to be so happy!"

Charlie wasn't quite smiling, but he was close to it as Ashleigh rode Silverjet to the winner's circle. Mike gave her a thumbs-up, which she returned. Samantha's lightly freckled face was glowing.

"That was a nice surprise," Charlie muttered as he took Silverjet's bridle. "Wasn't sure you had it in you, fella. You rode a good race, missy. Just like I wanted."

"Thanks, Charlie," Ashleigh said, catching her breath. "He really gave it all he had."

"At least I've got one winner this spring."

"You'll have more," Mike said quickly.

Charlie pushed back his hat. "Not with the bunch I'm training."

Ashleigh waited as the photographer snapped their picture, then she dismounted and removed the saddle to weigh in. "Don't forget about the auction tomorrow, Charlie. I just might find another Wonder."

Charlie snorted. "If I were you, I wouldn't get my hopes up too high. Like I said, the Smiths have some good stock, and you may find some bargains, but I haven't heard anyone getting that excited about what's being offered."

Ashleigh wasn't about to be discouraged. "No one was getting excited over Wonder either before we took her over."

"She was a once-in-a-lifetime filly," Charlie said shortly.

"We'll see." Ashleigh said with confidence.

When Ashleigh had changed out of her riding clothes, she joined the others back at the barn. "How'd he come out of it?" she asked Charlie.

"Pretty good. I'll hang around until he's cooled out, then van him back to the farm."

"We'd better get going," Ashleigh said. "I need to get Sammy home."

"I'll see you tonight," Mike told her. "I'll pick you up at about six thirty so we can get something to eat before the movie."

"I'll be ready," Ashleigh said.

Later, as Ashleigh wove down the road toward

Townsend Acres, Samantha spoke quietly. "I'd sure like to ride the way you do."

"Well, you can," Ashleigh responded. "I mean, I've never seen you ride, but you've got a good hand with horses—a feel for them. I started exercise riding at your age on Dominator, that bay gelding out in the pasture. You've seen him, haven't you? He used to be a darned good racehorse, and now we use him as a pleasure horse, or sometimes a pace horse. No one would mind if you rode him, and with enough practice—"

Glancing sideways, Ashleigh saw Samantha's eyes widen with surprise, then Samantha frowned and shook her head. "My father wouldn't let me."

"But why? Dominator's a safe mount. He'd never act up on you, and you said you know how to ride."

For a moment Samantha stared out the window without saying anything. Then she sighed and looked down at her hands. "Ever since my mother died . . . I guess you've heard about that—"

"Yes. I'm sorry," Ashleigh said softly.

"My father's been different since then," Samantha explained. "I understand that he's sometimes depressed—but he's started treating me like I'm five years old. He won't let me do anything. I've been riding forever, but he doesn't even let me ride the escort ponies anymore. He's afraid something might happen to me."

"If you want, I could tell your father how safe Dominator is, or maybe Charlie could talk to him," Ashleigh suggested.

"Maybe, but I don't think it will do any good," she said.

Now Ashleigh knew what was making Samantha unhappy. Ashleigh thought it was awfully unfair of Samantha's father not to let her ride anymore, and she wished she could think of some way to cheer her up. "You know," she said after a moment, "no one would mind if you brought friends to the farm. Is there anybody you'd like to invite?"

"Well, I hardly know the kids at my new school. And we've moved around so much that I've never been in any school long enough to make good friends."

"That must be hard."

Samantha shrugged. "I'm used to it."

Poor kid, Ashleigh thought. *She really must be lonely.* "How would you like to come to the auction with me tomorrow?" she asked, turning her car into Townsend Acres' drive.

"Thanks for asking, but I'm doing something with my father. It's his day off."

"I'll see you when we get back, then. Maybe I'll have a great new horse to show you."

Samantha smiled. "I hope so."

"Not too bad a crowd," Mike said as he, Charlie, and Ashleigh crossed the lawn in front of Smith Farm the next afternoon to the tent that had been set up for the auction. The bidding would take place inside, but first they'd have a chance to inspect the stock that would be auctioned.

"At least we won't have a lot of competition," Charlie said. "If there's anything worth buying, that is."

Ashleigh winked at Mike, and he grinned back. Charlie was determined to be his crusty self. They headed in the direction of the stable buildings. The better horses would be inside, although there were several mares and young foals in the paddock.

A number of grooms were inside the barns, ready to lead any horse out of its stall if a potential buyer wanted to inspect it more closely. No one with any sense would buy a horse without first checking its conformation, movement, and physical condition. The horses were separated by category—older horses in training, two-year-olds in training, yearlings, broodmares, and stallions. Ashleigh was really only interested in seeing the two-year-olds, because they were still in the early stages of training but old enough to begin racing. She, Mike, and Charlie found the right section, then went slowly from stall to stall.

"That gray doesn't look bad," Mike said as they peered in at a tall, lanky colt.

Charlie shook his head. "Take a better look. He's kneed in."

Mike leaned into the stall to take a closer look. "Right. I see what you mean."

They continued on, consulting their programs for a description and the family tree of each horse. Ashleigh paused outside the stall of a chestnut colt. She motioned to one of the grooms. "Could you bring him out, please?"

The groom nodded, took a lead shank from the wall, and unlatched the stall door. Ashleigh, Mike, and Charlie were silent as the groom led the horse up and down the wide aisle. After a moment, Charlie asked him to stop, and with his hands he carefully inspected the colt's legs and feet. He walked around the colt several times.

"Not bad," he said finally.

But Ashleigh was frowning. Something about the horse just didn't click with her, even if he had the same brilliant copper coat as Wonder. "I'll think about him. Thanks," she said to the groom.

"You're being pretty fussy," Charlie told her as they headed toward the last few stalls. "That colt ought to make a decent investment at the right price."

Ashleigh just smiled. "I'll know when I see the one I want."

Charlie shrugged and shook his head. "This isn't Townsend Acres, you know."

But then Ashleigh looked into the second-to-the-last stall down the aisle and stopped dead in her tracks. Her lips turned up in a smile, and her hazel eyes brightened. "I think she's the one," she whispered.

Beside the door to the filly's stall was a name plaque. "FLEET GODDESS," it read. The filly was a very dark bay, nearly black. The only mark on her glistening coat was a small, triangular white star on her forehead. The filly had a beautifully shaped head and intelligent eyes. Her legs were long and straight, and she seemed big for a filly, standing probably over sixteen hands high. In her heart of hearts, Ashleigh had really wanted to find another filly, and now she thought she had.

"Would you bring her out, please?" she said to the nearby groom. "What do you think?" she added to Charlie and Mike.

"Pretty animal," Mike said.

"Let's wait till we get a good look at her." Charlie scowled down at his program as the groom led the filly out. "Nothing great in her bloodlines— Battlecry–Miss Tess by Indian God. I've heard of her sire." He frowned and scratched his head. "Battlecry. He raced a few years back, mostly up north. I didn't know that he'd sired any foals. Horse came out of nowhere and died on the track after winning the Breeder's Cup . . . must have been the year before Wonder raced."

"I remember," Mike said with a sigh. "A real tragedy."

"The horse won some Grade 1 stakes, but he's unproven as a sire," Charlie added skeptically. "His winning streak could have been a freak, and there are no guarantees he passed his talent on to his foals."

Fleet Goddess's history intrigued Ashleigh all the more. The filly could present a real challenge— just as Wonder had. Ashleigh kept her eyes on Fleet Goddess as the groom walked her up and down the aisle. She couldn't find a single thing wrong. The filly's conformation was nearly perfect. Her movements were smooth, yet she had plenty of muscle where she needed it.

The groom stopped the horse, and Charlie ran his hands over her legs, down her back, and over her powerful hindquarters. He checked her feet and teeth. Finally he shrugged. "Can't see anything wrong with her."

Ashleigh smiled. She'd made up her mind. This was the horse she wanted. She ran her hand over the filly's neck and touched her soft nose. The filly huffed a warm breath onto Ashleigh's palm, then threw up her head. Ashleigh was sure. She liked the filly's temperament, too— alert, but polite. She didn't have Wonder's sweet, trusting gentlencss, but then, she didn't know Ashleigh yet.

Ashleigh thanked the groom as he took Fleet Goddess back to her stall. It was almost time for the auction to begin, and people were heading out to the tent.

"Better get moving," Charlie said. "She won't be in with the first set, but I'd like to get a feel for how the bidding's going."

"All right," Ashleigh said, following Charlie and Mike toward the barn door. But then she noticed a woman hovering around Fleet Goddess's stall. "Wait," she said, pulling on Mike's hand. "Mike, look. That woman's asking the groom to bring Fleet Goddess out."

"Well, maybe she'll decide she doesn't want her," Mike said.

"Yeah, maybe," Ashleigh said, biting her lip. "I guess I should just wait and see what happens."

Mike and Ashleigh hurried after Charlie.

"So you've definitely decided on her?" Mike said to Ashleigh as they left the barn.

"You think I'm making a mistake?" Ashleigh asked.

"I didn't say that." He laughed. "Besides, if you've made up your mind, nothing I say is going to change it."

They set out toward the sign-up table outside the tent to get a bidding number. A short line was forming. Charlie saw someone he knew and went over to talk to him. "See you inside," he told Ashleigh and Mike.

"I'm glad Charlie's here," Ashleigh said to Mike as they took seats in the second row. Ashleigh put her bag on the chair next to her, saving it for Charlie. "This is my first auction. I'm not even sure what to do."

"Don't worry. Charlie and I will help you out."

A moment later Charlie appeared. "Found out a little more about the filly," he said as he sat down. "The Smiths bought her as a yearling at the Fasig-Tipton sale in Saratoga. Paid fifteen thousand for her. Anyway, her sire only covered three mares, and that was because he jumped the paddock fence one night. The breeders kept the other two foals, who were out of better mares, and sold this one. The other two foals are in training in New York. Too early to tell if they're going to do much at the track." Charlie settled in his chair.

"Fifteen thousand?" Ashleigh groaned. "I can't go that high."

"Probably won't have to. Prices aren't likely to go that high today. Anyway, the filly's not ready to race yet. Smith's trainer says she's coming along nicely, but he wasn't planning on racing her till fall. I wouldn't put too much stock in his word, though. He's not going to say anything negative with the filly on the auction block."

"How high should I bid, Charlie?"

"Up to you. It's your money."

Mike nudged Ashleigh and whispered in her ear, "If Charlie didn't like the horse, he'd tell you flat out. He must think she's got some potential."

"I know," she said. But Ashleigh wasn't sure she was making the right decision. She really wanted the filly, but she didn't want to make a foolish mistake, either.

The auction began, with the auctioneer banging his gavel to get everyone's attention. Ashleigh glanced around and saw the tent was barely half full. As the first horses were led out, she paid close attention to bloodlines and prices. The bidding was low. A very good yearling went for half of what Ashleigh had expected.

Then the two-year-olds were led out. There was some intense bidding for the first half-dozen horses, and Ashleigh was beginning to feel less and less optimistic about being able to afford Fleet Goddess. But then interest seemed to taper off again, and several buyers left the tent. Fleet Goddess's hip number was called. The auctioneer tried to start the bidding at ten thousand, but received no response. He dropped the opening bid to three thousand, and Ashleigh was about to thrust up her bidding number.

"Hold out, missy," Charlie said softly. "Let them fight it out. No need to bid till the end."

Ashleigh nodded, but it was almost impossible for her to sit still. Her stomach was flip-flopping nervously. What if someone else got the filly?

The bidding was up to seven thousand. Ashleigh could go to ten, but that was her absolute limit. She bit her lip and tried to be patient. The bids crept up by halves—seven thousand, seventy-five hundred, eight thousand. Then it suddenly stopped.

"I have eight thousand," the auctioneer called. "Who'll make it eighty-five? Do I hear eighty-five? Anyone? Finished at eight thousand?"

"Now," Charlie said.

Ashleigh raised her bidding card.

"Eighty-five!" the auctioneer cried, and continued his singsong. "I have eighty-five. Let me have nine thousand. Can I have nine?" Ashleigh's eyes swept the audience and landed on the woman who had been inspecting Fleet Goddess in the barn. The woman raised her card. "Thank you, I have nine thousand!" the auctioneer announced. "Do I hear nine thousand five?"

Ashleigh raised her card.

"I have ninety-five. Ten, anyone? Do I hear ten?"

Ashleigh held her breath. If someone raised the bid once more, she'd have to drop out of the bidding. She couldn't go higher than ten thousand.

"Ninety-five hundred once . . . ninety-five hundred twice . . . sold! To number twenty-three!"

Slowly Ashleigh lowered her card. The filly was hers! She couldn't believe it!

"Looks like you own another filly, missy," Charlie said.

Mike squeezed Ashleigh's shoulder. "Congratulations!"

SAMANTHA AND HANK WERE IN THE STABLE YARD WHEN Ashleigh, Mike, and Charlie pulled up in the one-horse van. The old groom had taken a liking to Samantha and had volunteered to show her around the stables.

"So, did you find anything?" Hank asked as Ashleigh climbed out of the cab of the pickup.

Ashleigh flashed a smile. "A filly. Wait till you see her!"

"A filly!" Samantha exclaimed, running to the back of the van. She watched wide eyed as Ashleigh unlatched the van door and backed Fleet Goddess down the ramp.

Once the filly was off the ramp, she immediately flung up her head and eyed her new surroundings. She flared her delicate nostrils as she sniffed the air. Then she snorted and pranced on slender legs as Ashleigh led her away from the van.

"Not bad," said Hank. "Got a nice look to her. She's a big filly."

Ashleigh noticed that Samantha's green eyes were sparkling with admiration as she studied the horse.

"What's her name?" Samantha asked.

"Fleet Goddess."

"Got her for a decent price," Charlie put in gruffly. "Wasn't much of a crowd."

"See anything else you liked?" Hank asked.

"Naw. Nothing special."

Ashleigh's parents and Rory were hurrying up the drive. Rory rushed ahead and stopped a few strides away from the filly, who'd started at his sudden approach.

"Easy, girl," Ashleigh soothed, rubbing her hand over the filly's muzzle. "What do you think, Rory?"

"She's as good looking as Wonder—but I bet she won't race as well," he said loyally.

"Maybe not, but if she does even half as well, I won't be disappointed." Ashleigh waited nervously for her parents' response. She'd had to plead with them to let her use the money, so she wanted their approval.

"I think you did all right," Mr. Griffen said. "Of course, I didn't think Mike or Charlie would let you buy a nag."

"I wouldn't have bought a nag even if I was by myself!" Ashleigh protested.

"I know you wouldn't," her father said, grinning, "but Charlie and Mike *do* have a little more experience with buying horses."

Mrs. Griffen went over to Fleet Goddess and gave her a closer inspection. "Beautiful conformation," she said. "And she looks the picture of health. Even if she doesn't do much on the racecourse, she should make a good broodmare."

"She's going to do great things on the racecourse," Ashleigh said firmly. "I feel the same way about her as I did about Wonder. I can't wait to start training her."

Charlie shook his head. "Don't start counting chickens before they're hatched. We're not even sure how far along in training she is." He pursed his lips. "Her sire was a real late bloomer. Barely lifted a hoof until he was four or five. Then he burned up the tracks."

"You know the sire?" Mr. Griffen asked.

"Only by word of mouth. I never saw him. He was a big black, so the filly takes after him in looks. Heard he was a tough one to train."

Mrs. Griffen turned to Ashleigh. "Excited?"

Ashleigh nodded. "And happy. I've missed not having a special horse of my own to train."

After the others had drifted off and Mike had set out for home, Ashleigh settled Fleet Goddess in a roomy box stall in the training stable. She talked softly to the filly as she gave her a light grooming to help her feel more relaxed in her new surroundings. Fleet Goddess was still a little on edge from all the excitement, but she seemed to be gradually calming down.

Ashleigh didn't even hear Samantha come up

the aisle until she saw the girl's red head over the stall door.

"Finished for the day?" Ashleigh asked.

Samantha nodded. "I gave Hank and one of the other grooms a hand feeding the horses. It must be an incredible feeling to have your own racehorse," Samantha added after a moment.

"It's pretty exciting," Ashleigh said. "But buying my own horse makes me a little nervous, too."

"Why? I've seen you handle the horses. I think you'll do a great job."

"Well, a lot can go wrong. What if my training stinks, or she turns out to be a dud?"

"She won't. I get feelings about horses. . . ." The look on Samantha's face was intense. "She's going to be good."

Fleet Goddess turned her head and looked at Samantha. Then the filly gave a low whicker.

"I think she knows you're talking about her," Ashleigh said.

"See? She's smart, too."

"I've been thinking," Ashleigh said. "She's going to need some work on the trails, and I'll need someone to ride with me. Did you talk to your father about riding Dominator?"

Ashleigh instantly knew the answer from the troubled expression on Samantha's face. "It didn't do any good," Samantha said.

"That's a bummer . . . I'm sorry. But I bet he'll change his mind eventually."

Samantha frowned, and Ashleigh decided then

and there that *she* was going to talk to Ian McLean. Somehow she'd make him change his mind.

Ashleigh felt a touch of the jitters the next morning as she finished tacking up Fleet Goddess for her first workout. "Got that girth good and tight?" Charlie asked. "She's in a new place and may act up a little."

Ashleigh slipped her fingers under the girth of the saddle. It was tight, but not pinching, and she'd check it again once she mounted.

"Let's go, then," Charlie said. He shuffled ahead of Ashleigh as she led Fleet Goddess out of the stable. The morning air was crisp, and Fleet Goddess huffed excitedly once she was outside. Her ears pricked forward as she looked ahead at the other horses being led to the track for their workouts. Ashleigh saw Samantha waiting by the rail of the training oval.

Ashleigh had told Charlie earlier that she was going to talk to Ian McLean about Samantha riding Dominator. Charlie had scowled. "Doesn't do to stick your nose in where it doesn't belong," he warned.

"But she's not happy," Ashleigh had protested.

"Things don't always go the way you want. You should know that yourself."

"Yeah, I do," Ashleigh had said with a sigh, but she intended to talk to Samantha's father anyway.

As they reached the gap to the oval, Charlie motioned to Samantha. "Hold her head for me while I give missy a leg into the saddle."

Samantha took Fleet Goddess's reins while Charlie boosted Ashleigh onto the filly's back.

"She's a lot taller than Wonder," Ashleigh said as she checked the stirrups and girth, then gathered up the reins.

"And she's a half-green two-year-old. Remember that when you're out there on the track," Charlie said. "Try to keep her nice and calm—but be prepared for anything. See how she jogs after you warm her up. No need to gallop her today."

Ashleigh nodded, but Charlie's advice seemed overly cautious to her. Besides, she wanted to make her own decisions and do a lot of the filly's training herself. Before she moved the filly toward the track, she rubbed a hand down the filly's silky neck. "We're just going to get to know each other today. That's all."

At the gap Ashleigh checked to see that the outside of the track was clear, then she moved Fleet Goddess counterclockwise up along the outside rail. The filly immediately grew excited and started to prance, craning her neck against Ashleigh's hold on the reins and eyeing the two other horses working faster along the inside rail. "Easy now. You've been on a training oval before." Ashleigh spoke in a soft and quiet tone, hoping to reassure the filly in unfamiliar surroundings. Ashleigh knew from experience that a horse was sensitive to a rider's voice, and Charlie always said a rider got more with sugar than with vinegar.

Fleet Goddess seemed to settle a little, but she was still tense and excited. Ashleigh gradually let her out to a trot, but she continued to keep the filly near the outside rail, away from traffic. After they'd lapped half the mile oval, Ashleigh noticed that the filly was still distracted. Her ears were flicking back and forth, and she kept trying to turn her head in to see the other horses.

By the time they'd finished lapping the track, Ashleigh was beginning to wonder just how much preliminary training Fleet Goddess had had. The filly seemed awfully green, but maybe she was just working off some of her high spirits.

Ashleigh decided to try her at a jog. First she made sure there was a clear opening closer to the rail and that no horses were working nearby, then she tightened her left rein and moved Fleet Goddess to the center of the track. She gave the signal to canter. The filly strode out, but Ashleigh knew immediately from the horse's off-balance stride that she was on the wrong lead. Instead of leading with her left foreleg, she was leading with her right and upsetting her balance around the left-hand turns. Ashleigh pulled Fleet Goddess back into a trot, then tightened her left rein and pressed her right leg hard against the filly's side. This time Fleet Goddess led out correctly.

Ashleigh settled into the rocking-horse gait of the canter, concentrating on the filly's movements. They were amazingly fluid for such a long-legged young horse. Ashleigh felt a building sense of satisfaction as they cantered down the backstretch. The filly was moving beautifully. Ashleigh was sure she'd made the right decision in buying Fleet Goddess, and she couldn't wait to hear what Charlie had to say.

Fleet Goddess moved easily into the far turn, showing her agility.

Then suddenly a horse galloped past close on their inside, catching Fleet Goddess totally by surprise. She seemed to shudder for a moment; then she half-reared. Ashleigh reacted instantly and managed to get the filly down on all fours again, but Fleet Goddess thrust her head forward against the bit, yanking the reins through Ashleigh's fingers. She gave a frightened whinny and tried to break into a gallop up the track.

Ashleigh's firm hold on the reins prevented the filly from surging forward, but before Ashleigh knew what was happening, Fleet Goddess suddenly veered out across the track—straight toward the outside rail!

Ashleigh hauled hard on her left rein, desperately trying to change the filly's course. But the filly's legs churned beneath her as she fought Ashleigh's hold. Ashleigh pulled even harder on the reins. She had to keep Fleet Goddess away from the rail! Not only was there the danger of the two of them crashing into it, but Ashleigh saw Maddock, Mr. McLean, Charlie, Samantha, and a half dozen other staff grouped on the other side.

Ashleigh dragged with all her might on the left

rein. She had to change the angle of Fleet Goddess's panicked flight. She had to at least avoid the spectators, in case they couldn't back away from the rail in time. Frantically she considered her options. They were either going to crash through the rail or she'd have to get Fleet Goddess to jump over it.

She prayed that Fleet Goddess would have the sense to jump. But nothing was certain with a confused and terrified animal. Out of the corner of her eye, Ashleigh saw the shocked and fearful expressions on the faces of trainers, grooms, and riders. Fleet Goddess was only a few strides from the rail. With one last pull on her left rein, Ashleigh just managed to angle the filly past the crowd. But they were still heading for the rail.

Ashleigh tried to fight back her own panic as she saw the rail rushing toward them. She tried to steady herself in the saddle, lifting off slightly to encourage Fleet Goddess to jump. A stride away from the rail, she squeezed hard with both legs on the filly's sides and slid her hands forward, giving Fleet Goddess rein. The filly continued forward at the same mad pace, and Ashleigh's heart lurched.

"Jump!" Ashleigh said through gritted teeth. Then suddenly Ashleigh felt the horse gather her powerful hindquarters. In the next instant, they were flying over the rail and racing away from it. Ashleigh nearly fainted with relief.

"Oh, my God, we're over!" she cried. But now she had an out-of-control horse galloping toward the stable yard. She tried to circle the filly to slow her down, but Fleet Goddess wasn't responding to any guidance from the reins. She thundered forward over the dew-covered grass.

"It's all right, girl . . . all right . . . You don't have to be afraid . . . Slow down . . . Whoa . . . Whoa . . ." Ashleigh said the words as calmly as she could, and the filly's ears flicked back briefly, listening to her voice. Gradually the soothing words began to take effect. Fleet Goddess slowed her pace slightly, and Ashleigh finally managed to circle until the filly dropped down to a canter, then a trot, and finally to a shuddering walk. Charlie, Maddock, Mr. McLean, Samantha, and several exercise riders rushed over.

Fleet Goddess's sides were heaving, sweat drenched her dark coat, and her ears flicked nervously back and forth. Charlie was the first to reach them. He took Fleet Goddess's bridle and laid a gentle hand on her neck.

"Just take it easy, little lady. Everything's okay now. That's it."

Ashleigh saw the worried expressions on everyone's faces and suddenly she felt like she was twelve years old again—naive and inexperienced. She knew they were all thinking that she hadn't gotten much of a bargain in Fleet Goddess.

"It's not your fault," she whispered to the terrified filly. "Just relax." She noticed her own hands were trembling.

"Knew I shouldn't have believed the Smiths' trainer," Charlie barked.

"What happened?" Ken Maddock asked Ashleigh. "You're darned lucky neither of you was hurt."

"I don't think she's had any training on the track. I wonder if she's even been on an oval. . . . It scared her. I didn't realize . . ." Ashleigh let the sentence hang.

"You think she's that green? She showed some nice movement up until the time she fell apart," Maddock said. Ashleigh noticed that Mr. McLean was staring at them from a few yards away, his face drained of all color. The crazy ride probably reminded him of his wife's accident, Ashleigh realized. The same thing had happened to her, only his wife's mount had gone *through* the rail, not over.

Ashleigh quickly found Samantha in the crowd. The girl's face was pale too. Her freckles stood out in stark relief. *Oh, no,* Ashleigh thought. *I must have scared her half to death.*

"She's going to need some preliminary training," Charlie grunted. "Right back to the basics."

Ashleigh pulled her eyes away from Samantha. "I should have been better prepared, like you said." She groaned. She was feeling sick and guilty, too. What if someone *had* been hurt?

Charlie continued soothing the filly with gentle strokes of his hand. "Let's get her untacked and cooled out. Then you can start thinking about what comes next."

Ashleigh dismounted, quickly pulled up the stirrups and unfastened the saddle girth, then slid the saddle off the filly's steaming back. Ashleigh's legs felt like Jell-O, and she couldn't stop thinking about the expressions on Samantha and Mr. McLean's faces.

Charlie started leading Fleet Goddess off, and Ashleigh followed. She heard Maddock call from behind her. "That was a darn good piece of riding, getting her clear."

Ashleigh swung around, surprised. Ken Maddock nodded to her.

"Thanks," she managed to say.

5

AS SOON AS ASHLEIGH HAD REMOVED FLEET GODDESS'S bridle and put on her halter, she led the filly out to the yard to sponge off the sweat from her dark coat. The filly huffed with pleasure at the feel of the cool water on her steaming back.

Samantha had followed Charlie and Ashleigh back to the stable yard. She stood a few feet away, watching silently as Ashleigh worked and Charlie gave the filly another careful scrutiny. Ashleigh noticed that Samantha still looked a little pale, but she was watching the filly intently.

"Doesn't look like she's done herself any damage," Charlie said as he finished inspecting her legs. "She'll need a long walk, though, to cool her out. Wouldn't hurt to give her a good grooming and massage later, either."

"I'll walk her if you want," Samantha offered.

Ashleigh looked over at the girl. "Are you sure?"

Samantha nodded emphatically. "I'd really like to. I'll talk to her and calm her down."

Ashleigh could see that it was important to Samantha. And after the scare Samantha had had, maybe being with the filly was the best thing for her.

"Okay," Ashleigh said. "Thanks. I'll wait here and talk to Charlie until you get back." Ashleigh handed over Fleet Goddess's lead shank and ran a gentle hand down the filly's neck. "You've had a rough morning, haven't you, girl? You go off with Sammy. You'll feel better after a walk."

The filly bobbed her head, and Samantha led her off under the trees. Charlie motioned to a bench and told Ashleigh to sit down.

"Don't say it, Charlie," she said, grimacing. "I knew I goofed."

"Wasn't going to say anything of the sort."

"Do you think she spooked like that just because she's green?"

"I'd say that was a good part of it. The way she was behaving, even before she ran out, sure looked like she'd never been on a track before with other horses. It's probably a new scene for her. Anyway, she's had a lot of excitement the past two days. Might be a good idea to give her a day's rest, then take her out on the trails before trying her on the oval again."

"That's what I was thinking." Ashleigh dropped her head into her cupped hands. "When I do take her out on the oval again, I should do it when there aren't other horses working—maybe work her with Dominator, to settle her down."

"That's what I'd do," the old man said mildly. "Of course, she's your horse."

"Oh, Charlie, I felt so dumb this morning after she ran away—like I didn't know what I was doing! I'm beginning to see there's an awful lot I don't know about training. It's not going to be the same as training Wonder."

"No two horses train the same," the old trainer said. "They all have their little quirks and need a special hand."

Ashleigh lifted her head and looked at Charlie. "How'd you think she looked before she spooked? I know she was distracted early on, but once she started jogging down the backstretch, she felt good to me. Her movements were nice and smooth."

"Yup, they were. She's got a nice stretch of leg and good energy, but you and I both know that alone doesn't mean she'll turn into a good race-horse."

"Yeah, I know." Ashleigh rubbed her hands along her jean-clad legs, then rose. "I'll go see how Samantha and the filly are doing. Then I'd better get ready for school. Thanks, Charlie."

"No need to thank me."

"I'm going to be an hour or so late getting home tonight," Ashleigh added. "I'm staying to watch Linda's tennis match—but maybe I should change my plans and—"

"The filly will be fine. I'll keep an eye on her. Maybe I'll have Hank turn her out in the pasture for a few hours. She'd like that better than being cooped up in her stall."

Ashleigh felt better as she went to find Samantha and Fleet Goddess. When she caught up to them near one of the stable buildings, the filly seemed more relaxed, and the color had returned to Samantha's face.

"I think she's cooled out enough," Samantha said. "And she's calmer."

Ashleigh stroked the filly's neck and nodded. "I'll take her back to her stall and give her a grooming before school. Thanks again, Sammy. I think she likes you."

"Well, I definitely like her," Samantha said. "She didn't mean to go crazy this morning."

"I know she didn't," Ashleigh said, smiling. "She just needs a little more training. That's all."

After her last class, Ashleigh stashed her books in her locker, grabbed her lightweight jacket, and went out the back door of the high school building into the warm, late-April sunshine. She saw her friends Corey and Jennifer already seated on a bench next to the tennis courts.

"Hi!" Corey called out cheerfully. Corey was forever changing her hairstyle, and she had her short blond hair slicked back from her face. Jennifer, who had piled her long, honey-colored hair on top of her head, always looked spectacular. She was definitely the prettiest girl in their junior class, and the most popular with the boys.

Ashleigh slid onto the bench beside them. She saw Linda standing with the other girls on the tennis team on the far side of the courts and waved to her.

Corey leaned over. "How'd you do on that chemistry test?" she asked Ashleigh.

"Okay, I think," Ashleigh answered, "though there were a couple of tough questions on it."

Jennifer tossed her head. "Chemistry! I don't know how either of you can stand it."

"We need it for college," Ashleigh answered, "and it's not all that bad."

Jennifer didn't look convinced. "I'm glad I've decided to go into fashion design." Ashleigh and Corey laughed, then turned their attention to the tennis game.

Linda played furiously from the moment she served, but the teams were tied in the third set. Ashleigh saw the concentration on Linda's face as Linda dashed back and forth across the back court, returning the ball. Finally Linda connected with one of her powerful backhands, sending the ball skimming over the net. The opposing player couldn't get to it in time. The set was over, and Henry Clay had won!

All three girls jumped to their feet. "All right, Linda!" They hurried over to Linda to congratulate her and her partner. "Great match!" Ashleigh cried.

"I was getting a little worried in that last set," Linda said, "but we did okay. This puts us in the semifinals."

"That's great," Ashleigh said. "Hey, do you want

me to wait and give you a ride home?"

"Thanks, but one of the girls on the team said she'd take me. It'll take me a while to get cleaned up anyway. I'll see you in the morning, but call me tonight and let me know how the filly is."

"Okay. I will," Ashleigh said, waving as she backed away.

Ashleigh walked out to the parking lot with Corey and Jennifer. "See you tomorrow," Ashleigh called as she headed to her own car. Her thoughts wandered to Fleet Goddess as she drove away from the school complex. She knew Charlie was keeping an eye on her, but she was still concerned about the filly settling into her new surroundings. And, as always, she was anxious to see how Wonder's Pride was doing.

Ashleigh was whizzing along the main county road toward Townsend Acres when she saw Samantha walking along the grassy verge of the road. Her red hair shone in the sun like a beacon.

Ashleigh pulled her car over to the side, stopped, and waited. Samantha hurried up breathlessly.

"Could you give me a ride?" she asked.

"Sure. What happened? Why are you walking?"

"I missed the bus," Samantha explained as she slid into the passenger seat.

"Why didn't you call the farm? Someone would have picked you up."

Samantha looked down at her hands, then shrugged. "Actually, I had detention."

"Oh."

"I don't usually get detentions," Samantha said

angrily, "but a couple of kids started talking about me before history class—you know, behind my back—calling me a track brat. I lost it and told them off, and the teacher walked in then and gave me a detention."

Ashleigh knew that some people looked down their noses at anyone who lived on or near the backside of racetracks. "They must have been real jerks," she said. "I'm glad you told them off, but I don't think your father would have wanted you to walk the five miles home just because you got a detention."

"He'll be mad."

"But why? You were only standing up for yourself."

"He just will. He always tells me to watch my temper."

"Do you lose your temper a lot?" Ashleigh asked, trying not to smile.

Samantha shrugged again. "Only when I have good reason to."

"How are you liking school otherwise?"

"Oh, it's okay. Most of the kids are nice. It's just the snobs who bother me. I've never had any trouble at school—except for last year. And I usually get honors." Samantha flushed modestly.

"I think you should explain what happened to your father," Ashleigh said gently. "Why have him get angry with you for no reason?"

"Yeah, I guess."

"I'm going to be up at Fleet Goddess's stall later.

Come by when you've talked to him. Okay?"

"All right. I will."

Ashleigh still planned on talking to Mr. McLean about Samantha's riding Dominator, but after her near disaster with Fleet Goddess that morning, she had decided to wait for a while. She dropped Samantha off in the training area, then made her way toward Fleet Goddess's stall. The filly eyed Ashleigh as she looked over the stall door, then tore another mouthful of hay from her net.

"You're looking much better," Ashleigh said.

"Yup, she is better." Charlie had come up beside Ashleigh. "Spent most of the day in the pasture, and that seemed to take off the last of her nerves. You might want to give her another day before you take her on the trails, though. Better to be safe than sorry."

Ashleigh nodded in agreement. "I'll come back after dinner and take you for a walk," Ashleigh said to the filly. "See you later, Charlie."

Ashleigh got back in her car and parked it in her parents' driveway. She still had some time before dinner, so she hurried inside to call Mike.

"It's a good thing neither of you was hurt," he said after she told him what had happened that morning. "Charlie's right. Just be patient with her, and she'll turn out fine—though I know patience isn't one of your strong points."

Ashleigh could almost see him grinning. "I'll try," she said, laughing.

They talked a few minutes longer, and Mike said

he'd stop by the farm the next day. After they hung up, Ashleigh went out again to visit Wonder and Wonder's Pride.

On her way, she met Bill Parks coming out of the barn with a lead shank in hand.

"Perfect timing!" he called. "I was just collecting Wonder and the foal to bring them in the barn. Maybe you'd like to join me."

"Sure," Ashleigh said. She and Bill walked up to the white fence bordering the paddock and looked over. Wonder was holding her head up and looking in their direction. She immediately whinnied when she saw Ashleigh. She tossed her head so her silky copper mane flew, then whickered to her foal and set off toward the fence.

Wonder's Pride bounded after her. He had already grown an inch since his birth the week before, although he still seemed to be all legs and head as he scrambled after Wonder. He was definitely going to look just like her, Ashleigh thought.

Ashleigh sighed and smiled, then reached out a hand to rub Wonder's nose. Wonder's Pride stuck his own head between the slats of the fence and nudged Ashleigh's leg.

"You want some attention, too?" Ashleigh said softly as she lowered her other hand to the foal's fuzzy head and rubbed his oversize ears. "Ready to go in and eat, girl?" Ashleigh added to Wonder. "Come on down to the gate."

Ashleigh took a few steps to the railed paddock gate, which Bill unlatched. He handed her the lead shank, and she clipped it to Wonder's halter. Wonder eagerly stepped through, and Wonder's Pride followed, nearly tumbling over his legs in his haste to keep up with his mother. As Ashleigh led mare and foal to the barn, Bill latched the gate. "Thanks," Ashleigh called back over her shoulder.

"Feed's already in her stall," Bill said.

Wonder hesitated a second as they entered the darker barn, then whinnied to the other mares already in for the night. The foal skidded to a stop beside her and would have fallen on his rump if Ashleigh hadn't gripped him with a steadying hand. Once he had his balance again, they continued on to Wonder's stall.

Ashleigh led them in, unclipped the lead shank, and threw her arms around Wonder's neck. "You'll always be my favorite horse," she said. Wonder nuzzled her softly in return. Ashleigh leaned down to the foal and hugged him, too. He put up with her embrace for a moment, then playfully backed away through the thick bedding, tripped, and fell down. Ashleigh laughed as he struggled to his feet.

"See you two later," she said as she closed the stall door.

Ashleigh's parents were already in the kitchen with Rory when Ashleigh came in after washing up. As usual, Rory was sitting in the window seat, poring over a horse magazine. At twelve, he still shared Ashleigh's love of horses, though baseball and football were beginning to cut into that interest.

Rory put down his magazine when he saw

Ashleigh. "Hank told me what happened with the new filly this morning. Boy, I wish I had been there! Did she really jump the fence?" Rory had already left for the school bus by the time Ashleigh had returned to the house that morning.

"She did."

"Wow! Incredible."

"I'm just lucky she went over it instead of through it," Ashleigh said dryly.

"Yeah, I guess," Rory said. "But I still wish I'd been there. Exciting things like that don't happen very often."

"Thank heavens," Mr. Griffen said, taking a chicken out of the oven. "You were really lucky, Ashleigh. Charlie told me it took a good piece of riding on your part to keep her from crashing into the rail."

"Charlie said that?" Ashleigh smiled to herself. With Charlie, the compliments usually came secondhand.

"So the filly's a lot greener than you thought," her mother added. "It'll mean a tougher training schedule for you."

"I know." Ashleigh went to the refrigerator to get some water. "It doesn't look like she'll be ready to go near a racetrack until fall."

"Well, she'll keep you busy over the summer," Mrs. Griffen said. "Speaking of which, Caroline will be home soon. Her classes are over the second week in May."

"It'll be great to have her home," Ashleigh said.

Mrs. Griffen nodded. "But I don't think we can count on seeing too much of her. She called today and told me she's lined up a full-time job in Lexington working in an accountant's office. She says the pay won't be great, but it'll be good experience for her. And I imagine she'll be spending most of her evenings with Justin."

"Right," Ashleigh said, knowing her sister and her boyfriend of two years would be spending all their free time together. "Well, at least she'll be home. I miss having her yell at me about the mess on my side of the bedroom. And I'd better do some drastic cleaning before she gets here!"

Mrs. Griffen smiled. "I was going to suggest that."

"Great," Rory said. "I can't wait to hear you two screeching at each other again."

6

THE SKY WAS STILL LIGHT WHEN ASHLEIGH WALKED UP the stable drive after dinner. She loved the softness of the scenery as the last fading rays of sun turned the lush grass pastures into fields of emerald. In the dips between the low, rolling hills, a light mist was forming, drifting up to the still barely leafed treetops. She took a deep breath of the sweet, grass-scented air and felt lucky to be at Townsend Acres.

As she approached Fleet Goddess's barn, she saw Samantha standing beside one of the trees outside. Charlie, Hank, and several other grooms were sitting on a nearby bench, talking.

"Have you been to see the filly?" Ashleigh asked.

"Not yet. I thought I'd wait for you."

"Let's go, then. I want to take her out for a walk and see if she's moving all right."

When they had Fleet Goddess out on the wide,

grassy lane that led to the trails behind the stables, Ashleigh decided to ask Samantha about her talk with her father. "Did you talk to your dad?" she asked.

"Yeah. He was upset that I didn't call him, but he understood why I got angry." Samantha frowned. "He was angry, too, but he said next time I should just ignore the teasing and hold back my temper."

"He's right, but I know it's not easy. I told Brad off once when he got on my case—and was pretty sorry afterward. He made my life miserable and kept me from riding Wonder for a while."

"He *did*?" Samantha was astounded. She scowled. "He's not going to interfere with Goddess, is he?"

"He can't. She's my horse."

Ashleigh had been watching the filly as they walked, and she was reassured to see that the nearly black horse was moving with ease. She didn't seem to have hurt herself during her wild ride that morning.

Fleet Goddess arched her neck and whickered, then nudged Ashleigh's shoulder with her nose. "Yes, girl. We're going to turn you into a really good racehorse. It'll take time. And it's going to be hard work."

"I've watched lots of horses being trained. I know they don't always win—sometimes they don't even race." Samantha turned and studied the filly. "But Fleet Goddess is going to do both."

Ashleigh smiled. "You're that sure, huh?"

"She's a nice filly. And I don't care if people think her breeding's not all that hot."

"Who's been talking about her breeding?" Ashleigh asked curiously, knowing that a new horse in the stable, especially one that she'd bought herself to train, would mean gossip.

"Oh, some of the grooms. They don't think she'll do much."

Ashleigh laid a hand on Fleet Goddess's shoulder, then looked over to give Samantha a wink. "I've heard stuff like that before. I'll just have to prove them wrong, won't I?"

Two days later, Ashleigh saddled Fleet Goddess for her first ride on the trails around the farm. Charlie had agreed to ride out with her on Belle, the Appaloosa mare he often used as a mount. As they left the stable yard, Ashleigh noticed the wistful expression on Samantha's face. She felt bad for her, but she still didn't think it was the right time to talk to her father.

Fleet Goddess was full of high spirits. She danced along on her slender legs, tossing her head and snorting. Ashleigh sat deep in the saddle and kept the horse firmly in hand. "Just take it easy," she said in a soothing voice. "We're going to have fun today."

Charlie had Belle alongside, and the older mare's placid disposition seemed to steady Fleet Goddess. She settled into a prancing walk as they moved out of the stable yard and up along one of the grassy avenues between the paddocks.

"When we get to the top of the rise, we can trot 'em," Charlie said. "Get rid of her excess energy. Some long, easy works should do her good."

"Did you see the expression on Sammy's face when we rode out?" Ashleigh asked.

"I saw it." Charlie pursed his lips. "You ever talk to McLean about the girl riding?"

"No. It doesn't seem like a good idea—after he just saw Fleet Goddess spook."

"Give him time. He's got a lot on his plate right now settling in to the new job," Charlie advised. "Okay, let's trot 'em. Keep her well in hand."

Over the next few weeks Ashleigh and Charlie continued working Fleet Goddess on the trails. Gradually, with the easygoing Belle trotting beside her, Fleet Goddess was settling down and listening to Ashleigh's commands.

Every morning after her ride with Charlie, Ashleigh checked in on Wonder and her foal. Wonder's Pride was growing by leaps and bounds, entertaining everyone with his antics and already showing himself to be one of the dominant foals in the paddock. Of course, Wonder didn't take any nonsense from the other mares, either. She was first to push through to the water trough, and she laid back her ears, warning all the other mares to keep away until she'd finished drinking.

Caroline arrived home from college in the middle of May, a few days after Brad Townsend. On her first night home Caroline and Ashleigh talked as Caro unpacked. They caught up on all the news in each other's lives, then Caro asked, "So how's Brad?"

"The same." Ashleigh made a face. "Bossier, if anything. I'm not looking forward to having him back all summer." Two years before, Caro and Brad had dated, and it hadn't ended very well, though Ashleigh knew Caro was long since over it.

Caro laughed at Ashleigh's expression. "Is he still going out with the same girl?"

"I don't know. He hasn't brought her around here if he is. Frankly, I don't know why *any* girl would want to go out with him."

"Because he's cute and he's loaded. And he's not all bad," Caroline admitted.

"Can't convince me."

"I hear Mike has Jazzman entered in the Pimlico Special next weekend," Caro said as she carefully folded and put away several pairs of jeans.

"And he's getting pretty nervous," Ashleigh said. "Though I think Jazzman has a good chance of winning."

"Are you going up to Baltimore with Mike?"

Ashleigh grinned. "I sure am. I wouldn't miss it. Charlie and Samantha, the new assistant trainer's daughter, will keep an eye on Fleet Goddess for me."

"I have to get up to the training stables to see this new horse of yours," Caroline said. "You think she's going to be another Wonder?"

"You never know. She's a beauty."

"And all yours."

"And all mine." Ashleigh sighed.

Ashleigh walked into the stable the next afternoon to hear the echoes of a heated argument. She stopped in the shadow of the barn entrance to watch and listen. Brad and Samantha were standing outside Fleet Goddess's stall, and from the color on the girl's face, Ashleigh knew Samantha was furious.

"What is this animal doing in one of my stalls?" Brad stormed. "I want her out of here!"

"You're not moving her anywhere!" Samantha shouted back. "Not unless Ashleigh's told first."

"When did we start running a boarding stable around here?" Brad sneered.

"Goddess has had this stall since Ashleigh bought her."

That really set Brad off. Ashleigh could practically see the smoke coming out of his ears. He'd already left to return to college the Sunday Ashleigh had brought Fleet Goddess home, and this was his first visit back to the stables since then. "What makes the breeding managers' brat think she has a say in the running of this stable?" he growled.

Brad's jaw was tight with anger. Then he turned on his heel and strode up the aisle toward the door at the other end of the barn.

Ashleigh immediately hurried toward Samantha, who was standing with her fists planted on her slim hips, glaring after Brad. Ashleigh nearly laughed at the sight of the feisty girl, but the situation was too serious for that.

"I heard," she said as she reached Samantha's side. "I'll talk to Mr. Townsend. He told me I could put Fleet Goddess in here."

Hank came over, frowning. "I knew there'd be fireworks as soon as he found out who the filly belonged to," he said. "Too bad Sammy here got in the middle of it."

"I had to say something!" Samantha shouted. "He just walks in here and says he's putting Goddess out in the pasture where she belongs."

"Yeah, I know Brad," Ashleigh said. "But you probably should have let me handle it. I don't like you getting caught in the middle."

"It's not like he needs the stall or anything," Hank said. "There are no new horses in the training area. If anything, we have more stalls than we need."

Ashleigh glanced in Fleet Goddess's stall and saw that the filly was pacing and snorting uneasily because of all the shouting. "Why don't you go in and calm her," she said to Samantha. "I'll go see Mr. Townsend."

Fortunately Brad had already left his father's office by the time Ashleigh arrived. Mr. Townsend looked up as she knocked on the open door. "Come on in," he said. "I think I know why you're here. Unfortunately I forgot to explain the situation with the filly to my son, so there were some mixed signals. You can leave her where she is. I'm going to be letting Brad take a bigger hand in the stable management, but I've already told him the filly can have that stall."

"Thanks, Mr. Townsend."

"And how's Wonder's foal coming along? I was going to go down and take a look at him. I think he's going to be our prize foal this year."

"He's doing great. He seems to get bigger every day."

"Have you come up with a name for him yet?" Mr. Townsend asked.

"I've kind of been thinking of him as Wonder's Pride," Ashleigh told him a little hesitantly.

Mr. Townsend cocked his head thoughtfully. "You know, I like that. Wonder's Pride. We won't have to file registration papers until late summer, but that sounds like a good name. Keep me posted on how your new filly's doing, too."

"Okay, I will," Ashleigh said. "And thanks again, Mr. Townsend." She turned and headed back to Fleet Goddess's stall.

7

SINCE MIKE HAD ALREADY LEFT FOR BALTIMORE WITH Jazzman, Ashleigh drove up to Pimlico with Mike's father. Mike was waiting for them when they arrived on Friday night. The track wasn't nearly as hectic as it would be the following weekend, when the Preakness, the second jewel in the Triple Crown, would be run, but there was still plenty of activity. The Pimlico Special was part of the American Championship Racing Series, and Mike was already getting the prerace jitters.

"He'll do great," Ashleigh assured him as they stood outside Jazzman's stall and inspected the coal black horse. The horse's coat shone with health, his muscles looked toned and taut, and his ears were pricked alertly. "You have him in perfect condition, and you said he had a really good workout this week. What are you worried about?"

"Wouldn't you be nervous if it were your horse racing?" Mike asked.

Ashleigh admitted she'd be in exactly the same state as Mike. "Yeah, I would. I'd be a basket case."

"So there," Mike teased.

Ashleigh grinned and took his arm.

"Come on, you two," Mr. Reese said with a smile. "Let's go get some shut-eye. You can't do anything more for him tonight, and I'm exhausted."

Ashleigh had a motel room next to the one Mike and his father shared. She slept like a log, but was wide awake at first light the next morning. They went straight to the track to see Jazzman, then had breakfast in the track kitchen, where they saw several other trainers who had horses entered in the race.

It took most of Ashleigh's energy to keep Mike calm until post time. He had so much riding on this race—both his horse and his reputation—and he had gone through a lot of disappointment the year before when injury had kept Jazzman out of the Triple Crown. She knew how important Jazzman's success was to him now.

Jazzman was in better shape than Mike when race time finally approached. Mike's old groom, Len, had the horse looking great, and Jazzman seemed to radiate confidence. Finally they led Jazzman to the infield of the track, where the horses would be saddled for the Pimlico Special.

Painted signs shaped like black-eyed Susans and

marked with the different post positions were set out on the grass. They went to number ten.

"I'm still not happy with this post position," Mike said as he prepared to tack up the horse.

"The way he runs off the pace," Mr. Reese told his son, "it shouldn't hurt him. And this way he won't get caught in the shuffle."

The black colt was a late closer with a big kick at the end—but Ashleigh knew anything could happen in a horse race. She glanced over at Mike's tight face. He was concentrating on getting the saddlecloth and saddle in place under the scrutiny of a track official.

Len led the gleaming animal off in a walk over the grass, and Julio Grazio, Mike's regular jockey, arrived at Mike's side. Mike gave the slim, dark-haired jockey some last-minute instructions. Then it was time for the jockeys to mount and head out onto the track for the post parade.

Mike, Ashleigh, Mr. Reese, and Len followed, along with the other trainers and grooms. They threaded their way across the track and up into the grandstand. "What are his odds now?" Mike asked, glancing up at the betting board. "Four to one," he said. "Well, I'm glad he's not the favorite. I've always felt that could be bad luck."

As they stood in front of their seats during the last anxious minutes before the start of the race, Ashleigh reached over and squeezed Mike's hand. He gave her a soft smile, then his eyes went back to the track as Jazzman was loaded.

A second later, the gate opened. Jazzman broke clean as a whistle, forging his way ahead without any urging, to settle in fifth. Grazio moved him in along the rail to save ground as the field rounded the clubhouse turn. He stayed in that position, even dropping back slightly, as the field made their way down the backstretch. The fractions for the first quarter and half mile flashed on the board. Twenty-three seconds for the quarter and forty-five seconds for the half. "Good, good," Mike muttered to himself.

The field moved into the far turn. Now was the time Jazzman would start making his move, shifting into overdrive and picking up horses as he swept past the field. But Jazzman was hanging. The leaders passed the quarter pole and he was still in fifth, ten lengths out of it.

Mike's grip on Ashleigh's fingers was so tight, she lost the circulation in them. "Kick in!" Mike cried through gritted teeth. "Come on! God, he's not going to make it!"

Ashleigh was feeling as anxious as Mike. If Jazzman didn't move soon, he'd never catch the leaders.

Then suddenly the horse was in gear. It was incredible to watch him start flying up along the outside of the field, sweeping by the other horses like they were standing still. They were into the stretch and Jazzman was in third, but he still had four lengths to make up to catch the leaders.

"Go!" Ashleigh and Mike screamed. "Go!" The horse was still moving like a speeding black blur.

He caught the leaders at the eighth pole, then lengthened his stride and, almost effortlessly, sailed past them. Grazio only showed him the whip once, then hand-rode the big horse as he increased his lead from a length to two lengths and swept under the wire to win by three!

"All right!" Mike cried, grabbing Ashleigh up in his arms and giving her a kiss. "What a race!" Mike's eyes were shining like blue sparklers.

"I told you he would do it," Ashleigh said, beaming.

Mr. Reese patted his son on the back and grinned from ear to ear. "That's a horse to make you proud. Good going, Michael!"

Mike took a deep breath and ran his hand over his forehead. "My God, I feel like I was out there running the race myself."

Ashleigh laughed. "From the way you were jumping up and down when he was coming down the stretch, I think you were."

"Oh, wow," Mike said, shaking his head in disbelief. "Let's get down to the winner's circle."

The excitement over Jazzman's win didn't quiet until they were on their way to Kentucky again. Mike had been mobbed by reporters. Ashleigh remembered the dizzying barrage from Wonder's big races. She had always loved all the attention, but this was Mike's day—and he deserved it.

Mike brought Ashleigh back to Townsend Acres on Sunday night, while his father drove the van carrying Jazzman back to Whitebrook. Together Ashleigh and Mike went to see Charlie and tell him the good news.

"Yup, watched the race on TV," the old trainer said gruffly. "Good effort. He come out of it okay?"

"In great shape, like he hadn't even been out on the track."

"Hmm. Guess you'll be heading for the Nassau County Handicap." As he spoke, Ashleigh noticed that Charlie seemed distracted, his mind not entirely on what they were saying.

"Has something been happening here?" Ashleigh asked, wondering if that's what was bothering Charlie.

"Nothing much. I had the McLean girl take the filly out for a walk. That's about it."

"I was thinking of trying Fleet Goddess on the oval tomorrow," Ashleigh said, "if you or one of the other riders could take out Dominator. After the way she's been working on the trails these last two weeks, I think she's ready."

"We'll arrange something," Charlie muttered.

Charlie had both Fleet Goddess and Dominator tacked up and waiting by the oval the next morning. One of the exercise riders, Johnny Byard, was standing with him.

"Maddock is going to have a late start," Charlie said. "We might as well work the filly before the other horses get on the track. Johnny will ride Dominator."

"Sure." Ashleigh smiled at Johnny, who had

been working at the farm for the last six months. Then she went over to Dominator. "Hi, old buddy. You going to keep the filly in line today?" The horse rubbed his head against Ashleigh's arm and whuffed through his nose. "I know, you always do a good job." Ashleigh wondered why Charlie wasn't riding Dominator himself, but figured that the old trainer just wanted to watch the filly work.

Ashleigh settled in the saddle and collected the reins. By now, Fleet Goddess knew her rider well. She was full of high spirits, but was playful rather than high strung. Still, Ashleigh couldn't help feeling a little anxious, remembering their last trip to the oval.

She looked over at Johnny, who was in Dominator's saddle. The big bay horse was standing by quietly. "I guess you were here the last time she was on the oval," Ashleigh said.

Johnny gave her a crooked smile. "Yeah. Green as heck."

"If you could keep Dominator outside of her, we'll just take it slow a few times around at a trot, maybe a jog. See how it goes."

"Gotcha." Johnny nodded, then he and Ashleigh moved the two horses onto the track.

Fleet Goddess's head was up, and she huffed excitedly several times as they moved through the gap onto the harrowed dirt. "Just take it easy, girl," Ashleigh soothed. "This isn't going to be like last time."

Johnny kept Dominator apace of Ashleigh and

Fleet Goddess as they crossed the track closer to the inside rail. He settled the gelding outside of Fleet Goddess. The filly was definitely distracted, so Ashleigh held her on a tight rein. The filly arched her neck as she fought the pressure.

Ashleigh glanced over at Johnny and nodded, and they simultaneously picked up the pace to a trot. They'd nearly lapped the track when Fleet Goddess finally put her mind to business and accepted the presence of a strange horse at her side. Dominator, old pro that he was, moved smoothly along in tune with his rider.

They continued at a trot for another lap.

"She seems to be moving okay," Johnny called over to Ashleigh. "Want to try a jog?"

Ashleigh debated for a second. She didn't want to push the filly too soon and risk another run out, but with Dominator there at her side, she felt safer. She nodded. "Let's go for it—just one lap."

Together Ashleigh and Johnny gave the horses the signal to canter. The filly exploded and nearly pulled Ashleigh's arms from their sockets as she tried to break straight into a full gallop. Ashleigh reacted instantly, tightening her grip on the reins and hauling back an inch. The filly resisted, but Ashleigh's firm check on the reins kept her to a canter.

She fought Ashleigh every inch of the way. It took all Ashleigh's strength to hold her. By the time they came off the backstretch into the final turn, Ashleigh's arms and shoulders were aching. As they neared the mile marker, she glanced over at

Johnny and shook her head, telling him that one lap was enough.

He immediately slacked off, but pulling the filly up involved another battle of wills. They'd gone a half-dozen strides past the marker pole before the filly finally relented.

"Heck, she nearly pulled you out of the saddle!" Johnny said as he rode up beside her. "That filly wants to move out."

"Not until she learns to stay *inside* the oval," Ashleigh said. "She would have tried to run out on me again if you hadn't been there."

"I kind of figured as much. But a few more trips like this with Dominator and she should settle down."

"Let's hope."

Samantha went to Fleet Goddess and held the reins as Ashleigh dismounted and pulled up the stirrup irons.

Charlie squinted at the filly. "She was pretty rank. Looked like she was trying to pull your arms out of their sockets."

"She didn't want to settle."

"Hope you don't have a fighter on your hands." Charlie pushed back his hat and scowled. "I gotta get back to the barn. My three-year-old looks like he's bruised his foot. I won't be working the rest of them this morning."

"But—" Ashleigh began. Charlie had already shuffled off.

"See ya," Johnny said as he led Dominator back

to the stable. Ashleigh looked over at Samantha and frowned. "Charlie's acting strange. Stalker's racing this weekend. He needs to be worked."

"That's what I thought," Samantha answered. "And he was pretty tough on Goddess. I mean, she's still learning."

"Tougher than usual," Ashleigh agreed.

"He was acting strange all weekend, too—just sort of sat around on the bench. He didn't work any of his horses much. He said the rest wouldn't hurt them, but that can't be true if Stalker's racing."

Ashleigh's frown deepened.

"Maybe he's not feeling well," Samantha suggested.

Ashleigh had been thinking the same thing, but Charlie probably wouldn't tell her if he was sick even if she asked him.

That afternoon when Ashleigh went back up to the training stables after school, Hank came up to her. "I don't know what's with Charlie, but I'm kind of worried about him," he said. "Nearly bit my head off this afternoon, and then instead of sitting down for our regular chat, he heads off to his room. Something's wrong. He told me he had some bug, but I think it's more than that. I've known him a long, long time. He's had colds and flu like the rest of us, but this is different."

"You don't think he's just in a bad mood?" Ashleigh asked.

Hank rubbed his bristly chin. "Nope. He may be hard as nails, but the last few days he's looked like heck, and he's not getting any younger. I think he should see a doc. Problem is getting him there."

"I can drive him to Lexington," Ashleigh offered quickly.

"But how're we going to get him to agree to go?" Hank asked.

"Maybe if Mr. Townsend suggested it?"

"Hmmm. Let me talk to Charlie first. Don't want to get his back up. I'll go see him now. You going to be here for a while?"

"I'll be right in the stable."

When Hank was gone, Ashleigh went into Fleet Goddess's stall and started grooming the filly. Samantha came up a moment later. "I heard what Hank said," she told Ashleigh, "and he's not the only one who's worried. A couple of the other grooms were talking."

"I just hope Hank can talk him into going to the doctor," Ashleigh sighed. "Something must be wrong if everyone's noticing." Ashleigh didn't want to think of anything being wrong with Charlie. Charlie had been the only one to offer his help with Wonder when she'd needed it the most. He'd taught her nearly everything she knew. If anything happened to him . . . she couldn't think of that.

Hank appeared a few minutes later. "He must know it's more than the flu," he said. "He doesn't have a regular doctor, but he agreed to let you drive him to the emergency room clinic. He'll be ready in a minute."

"I'll run down and get my car!" Ashleigh patted

the filly, stowed her brushes, and jogged down the drive.

Charlie protested all the way to Lexington that they were making a big deal out of nothing. Ashleigh didn't argue with him, but one look at his nearly white face told her something was wrong. After Charlie was led off to one of the examining rooms, Ashleigh watched the clock, getting more and more nervous. All day during school she'd been a little down about Fleet Goddess's lousy workout that morning. But suddenly, it didn't seem very important anymore. She looked again at the clock. Over an hour had passed. Why were they keeping Charlie so long? What was wrong? She fidgeted and chewed on a nail. Charlie was old, she knew, but somehow she'd expected him to be around forever.

Finally, when she'd made up her mind to go to the nurses' station and ask about him, Charlie appeared. His floppy hat was already on his head. Ashleigh jumped to her feet and hurried over. "Are you all right?" she cried. "What did they say?"

Charlie had a couple of slips of paper in his hand. "Gave me some pills to take," he said brusquely.

"That's all? But you were in there so long."

"Plugged me into these dumb machines, poked a bunch of needles in my arm. Say I'm run down, doing too much—hmph!"

"Maybe you have been doing too much."

"No more than I've always done—except for those couple years when they put me out to pasture. You know where there's a drugstore?"

"Right around the corner," she said quickly.

Charlie lapsed into silence. Ashleigh noticed his lips were pursed and his brow was furrowed, but she didn't question him any further. She offered to get his prescriptions filled for him, but he said he'd do it himself and walked slowly into the store.

When he came out and Ashleigh headed the car toward home, he still said nothing. He finally spoke when they were halfway to the farm. "Guess I'll have to get you and McLean to take over my horses for a few weeks."

Ashleigh gave him a startled look.

"Doctor doesn't want me doing anything except sitting in the sun. Bah!" he growled.

"I'll help," Ashleigh said immediately. But she knew it wasn't a good sign that Charlie had agreed to give up his training duties.

Charlie made another grunting noise, then sank into silence.

Hank was waiting when Ashleigh parked in the stable drive. Several of the other grooms were in the yard, too, and they all looked over curiously at Charlie when he stepped out of the car. Charlie nodded to them but made no comment, and went straight to his small apartment.

Hank looked over at Ashleigh. "What happened?"

Ashleigh repeated the little Charlie had told her.

"Complete rest, eh?" Hank said, frowning. "Doesn't sound good. I'll go up and see him in a while. He'll probably want to have a word with Ian McLean, but I'll leave that for him to decide. You don't want to interfere much with Charlie."

Jilly hurried over as they were talking. She'd just gotten back to the farm from the track. "I heard about Charlie," she said breathlessly. "What's up?"

Again Ashleigh explained, and Jilly's face grew serious. "I hope it's not a major illness. He's got to be near seventy."

"Probably just over," Hank put in.

"Well, he's definitely not young anymore," Jilly said worriedly, "and he's not easy on himself. Charlie just *doesn't* voluntarily take doctor's orders."

"Yeah, I know," Ashleigh said.

"I'll keep an eye on him," Jilly said firmly. "I don't want anything happening to that old guy. Don't worry, I won't let him know I'm nursemaiding him, and I think I'll be needing some advice on my upcoming races, anyway."

Hank smiled. "Yup. Trick him a little—not that the old fox won't see right through it."

Ashleigh returned to the stable after dinner. It was a warm May evening, and Charlie was sitting on a deck chair outside his apartment. He looked very relaxed and rested, but as Ashleigh drew closer, she saw that his face still looked gray and drained.

He motioned to her. "I talked to McLean," he said when she reached his side. "He said he'd be willing to fill in for a couple of weeks. Told him you knew the horses and what I wanted. He'll meet you in the stable in the morning. Stalker's going to need a good work this week."

Ashleigh nodded. "I think I've got a pretty good

idea of all the horses' training schedules, but I'll ask you if I have any questions."

Charlie was scowling. Ashleigh knew how he would hate being idle.

"Charlie, you'll be feeling great again in a couple of weeks, so don't worry. You took the pills the doctor gave you?"

"Don't start treating me like a baby," he barked, suddenly sounding like his old self. "It's bad enough Jilly and Hank are coddling me like an invalid—and then Townsend has to come over tonight and put in his two cents about my resting up!"

Ashleigh cringed. "Sorry," she murmured.

"Humph!" Charlie glowered.

8

THE NEXT MORNING WHEN ASHLEIGH ARRIVED AT THE stable, she found Mr. McLean alone with Hank. They were talking outside Charlie's row of stalls.

Mr. McLean smiled at her. "Morning."

"Good morning," Ashleigh answered. She was a little uncertain about training Charlie's horses with Mr. McLean. Everyone on the farm seemed to like him, but Ashleigh didn't really know him that well. And Samantha wasn't waiting in the stable like she usually was, which Ashleigh thought was strange.

But Mr. McLean was soft-spoken and friendly as he asked about the training schedule of each of Charlie's mounts. "You've been working with them," he said, "so you know their quirks and habits better than I do."

He listened carefully as Ashleigh told him what she knew of each of the six animals. "Well, Charlie's been aiming Stalker, the two-year-old, toward a maiden race next weekend. So he'll be due for a good gallop. Silverjet's in regular training. He won a claiming race a few weeks ago, but he needs to be placed in the right race . . ."

"Sounds good to me," Mr. McLean said when she was finished. "We'll work three of them today and three tomorrow. That'll give me time to deal with my own horses. I guess we can get Stalker saddled up now. After that take out the other bay, then the gray."

By the end of the morning, Ashleigh was beginning to see what a good trainer Mr. McLean was. He treated the horses right, understood what worked best for each of them, and frequently asked her opinion. The only time she saw him looking uptight was when Stalker, full of high jinks, tried to buck her off at the beginning of his workout. Ashleigh held on like glue, and the colt soon settled down, but Mr. McLean's expression was tense until the workout was over.

Still, the morning had gone well enough that Ashleigh decided it was a good time to ask him about allowing Samantha to ride. She waited until he'd checked Stalker over, then spoke as calmly as she could, even though she was a little nervous about bringing up the subject. "I was wondering," she said. "I'm going to be needing some extra help with my filly, especially now that Charlie's sick. Sammy's told me she's a good rider, and I thought she could ride along with me on Belle or Dominator, like Charlie's been . . ."

Before she had even finished the sentence, she saw Mr. McLean's face tighten. He gave a quick shake of his head. "No," he said harshly, then tried to soften his tone. "I really don't think Sammy's ready to do any exercise riding."

"It wouldn't be on the oval," Ashleigh assured him. "Just on the trails, and Belle and Dominator are totally safe."

He was silent for a second. Ashleigh could see the pain on his face, as if he were remembering his wife's terrible accident. "I don't think so," he said with finality. "She's too young. I don't want anything to happen to her." Then he shook his head as if clearing it. "I'm sure you'll be able to work something out," he added in a more helpful tone. "A lot of the regular exercise riders have some free time now, you know. Well, I've got to go work my other horses. I'll see you tomorrow morning."

Ashleigh knew there was no point in calling after him. She could tell from his expression that he wasn't going to change his mind, and if she pressed him, it might only make him angry.

Jilly walked up as Ashleigh was dismounting. "Finished?" she asked.

"Last one," Ashleigh answered. "I'll take him back and turn him over to Hank."

"You're not working the filly this morning?"

"No. I thought things would be pretty confused, and I don't have a rider for Dominator."

"Hey, I'm going to be around for a few days. Would you like me to ride Dominator?"

"Would I ever!" Ashleigh cried. "That would be a big help."

"I get the feeling Sammy would really like to ride Dominator," Jilly said, looking over at Ashleigh. "Why doesn't she? She told me she used to ride all the time."

"Not since her mother was killed. Her father won't let her. I just talked to him about it."

"He's afraid of another accident, huh?" Jilly said sadly. "I suppose it's a pretty natural reaction."

"But it doesn't make Sammy very happy."

"I just saw her up in the barn with Fleet Goddess," Jilly said.

"Oh, is that where she is? I was wondering why she didn't show up for the workouts."

"She said something about finishing some homework she didn't get done last night," Jilly said.

"You know, I've been thinking about asking her to be Fleet Goddess's groom. She needs something important to do around here."

"Not a bad idea," Jilly said. "And she obviously loves that filly."

Ashleigh turned Stalker over to Hank, then went into the barn to find Samantha.

"You mean it? I can be her groom?" Samantha said, gaping at Ashleigh.

"I think you'd be great with her," Ashleigh said with a smile, "and you're already good friends."

Samantha's face lit up. "I'd *love* to be her groom. I'll do the best job in the world. I know what to do."

"I'm not worried about that, and I'll pay you."

"You don't have to pay me," Samantha said in amazement.

Ashleigh laughed. "It wouldn't be fair otherwise. I'll give you the same as the other beginning grooms get." Ashleigh didn't think her parents would object to her taking that small amount from her savings. "Do you want to start this afternoon? Goddess will need a walk since she didn't get worked this morning."

Samantha jumped up in the air with excitement. "Yes," she said, suppressing a squeal. "As soon as I get home from school."

"It's a deal, then," Ashleigh said.

Ashleigh couldn't believe how happy the offer had made Samantha. Seeing the younger girl's face brighten helped make up for Ashleigh's disappointing conversation with Ian McLean.

Amazingly, Charlie was sticking to doctor's orders, although he didn't have much choice with everyone watching him like a hawk, and it had only been twenty-four hours since he'd been to the hospital.

Ashleigh found him that afternoon where she'd expected he'd be, sitting on a deck chair in the sun where he could keep an eye on the stable activity. His color seemed a little better, though Ashleigh wondered if she was just seeing what she wanted to see. His mood hadn't improved any.

"Hear you didn't work the filly this morning," he said as soon as she walked up.

"I figured I wouldn't have time, and I'd forgotten to get a rider for Dominator. But Jilly's going to ride for the next few days."

"That so."

"Stalker had a good work this morning," Ashleigh said, trying to cheer him up.

"So I heard from McLean." He paused and pulled on his ear. "You like him?"

"He's a good trainer. He knows what he's doing and is really good with the horses. He's already picked up on all their quirks and knows how to work with them." Ashleigh hesitated. "I asked him about Sammy riding. He said no."

Charlie nodded. "Expected that."

"I'm not going to tell Sammy I asked him. He's still pretty upset about his wife's accident."

Charlie frowned.

"I've asked Sammy to be Goddess's groom," Ashleigh said in the growing silence.

"Yup. Good idea. The kid needs something to do. I see her moping around a lot." Hank walked over and gave Charlie a nod. "You're looking more like yourself," he said.

"Better be, the way I'm being babied."

Hank lowered his voice. "You hear that Townsend kid's stirring up more trouble now that he's home for the summer?"

"No, I didn't," Charlie answered.

"He laced into one of the young grooms over in the other barn this morning. Didn't like the way the groom was cleaning his tack. Turned out to be a real shouting match. The groom quit on the spot. Now they'll be shorthanded over there."

"At least he's found a couple of two-year-olds to keep him busy," Charlie said. "Heard he's been working them in the mornings himself."

"And won't listen to a word Maddock says, either."

So Brad was being obnoxious again, Ashleigh thought. At least he'd left Fleet Goddess alone, although Ashleigh didn't count on that lasting for long. She couldn't wait until July, when Brad left for Saratoga, where the Townsends had a second home near the track.

By early June Charlie had perked up a little. Although he still couldn't take an active part in training his horses, they were doing well under Mr. McLean's supervision. Stalker had run second in his maiden race, but only by a neck, and Charlie was pleased about that, though it was obvious he resented not being present at the colt's first race. Fleet Goddess had improved tremendously from the four works she'd had with Jilly and Dominator. She was learning not to lunge at the bit or to run out of the oval every time she was frustrated. In a few weeks, school would be out for the summer, and Ashleigh could hardly wait to have more time to work with the filly.

When Jilly left that week to ride at the Belmont racetrack in New York, Ashleigh asked Johnny Byard to ride Dominator. Johnny was just putting his foot in

Dominator's stirrup when Brad stormed up.

"What are you doing?" he asked Johnny.

Johnny gave him a blank look. "Riding. That's what I'm hired to do."

"Right," Brad said. "By me."

No one seemed to understand what was going on. Maddock and Mr. McLean looked over with surprise from where they were standing near the rail.

"And if you're hired by me," Brad added, "you'll ride *my* horses! That filly has nothing to do with this stable. She's only boarded here. You're not riding a pace horse with her. No one on my payroll rides unless I tell them to. Clear?"

Johnny shrugged. He gave Ashleigh an apologetic look and dismounted. "Okay by me, boss," he said sarcastically. He handed Dominator's reins to Samantha and walked off. Brad turned and walked off himself.

Ashleigh was furious. For the first time in a long while she acted without thinking and went right up to Brad. She found him saddling a horse outside the stable.

"Why?" she demanded with her hands on her hips.

Brad gave her a snide smile. He knew exactly what she was talking about. "You want someone to ride a pace horse, then hire your own rider. We're not in the charity business. Your filly's already taking up one of my best stalls rent-free and eating her head off."

"I'm paying for her feed, and your father doesn't mind my using one of the riders for a lousy fifteen minutes in the morning!"

Brad clenched his jaw. "When my father's away on business, and for as *long* as he's away, I'm in charge! I'm not giving you a rider for free like my father does. Use some of Wonder's prize money my father so generously gave you and pay your own rider's fees." Brad dropped the stirrup of the horse he was saddling, took the horse's reins, then looked back over his shoulder. "Don't expect any more special favors." He mounted and rode the horse off.

Ashleigh stared after him, too angry to get the words past her throat. But what had she expected from Brad? He'd never gotten over his jealousy of her and Wonder's accomplishments!

Sammy was standing by the ring, holding Fleet Goddess, when Ashleigh returned. Her green eyes were open wide. "What happened? Did you tell him off?"

"I sure did," Ashleigh growled. She knew everyone was staring at her—all the exercise riders and grooms and both the trainers, but she didn't care. She wanted to put Brad Townsend in a hole!

"So what's going to happen to Goddess's training?" Samantha asked.

"I'll work something out. Maybe Jilly can come back for a couple of days. Brad can't stop *her* from riding."

9

WHEN THE PHONE RANG LATE THAT SATURDAY AFTER-
noon after the Nassau County Handicap, Ashleigh raced from the living room to get it.

"Jazzman won!" Mike shouted from New York.
"Did you see it?"

"We sure did!" Ashleigh cried. "Linda, Sammy,
Caro, and I watched every second. He was great!
They can't doubt him now."

"Did you see that stretch drive? He was leaving them in the dust—and he equaled the second-
fastest track record, and it wasn't even a really
fast track." Mike was so excited, he could barely
talk straight. "I can hardly believe it!"

"I can," Ashleigh said. "I *told* you he was going
to win. He's a good horse and you're a good
trainer. How'd he come out of the race?" she asked.

"Good, really good. It didn't seem to take
much out of him at all. I hope to bring him back

home tomorrow night. I can't wait to see you."

"Can't wait to see *you*," Ashleigh said. "Call me as soon as you get in."

"I will," Mike promised. "Wait a minute, I almost forgot to tell you. I saw Fleet Goddess's half brother run today."

"You did?" Ashleigh said with interest.

"In a two-year-old maiden race. He's a big black called Son of Battle. Mean-running animal. He broke badly out of the gate and still won!"

"You're kidding. Really?" Ashleigh tried to absorb the news. She felt a surge of excitement—Goddess's brother was racing and winning. "Can you bring me home a copy of the race program and the *Daily Racing Form*?" she asked. "I want to find out more about him."

"I already picked up copies for you."

"So you really thought he was impressive?" Ashleigh asked. "Did he look anything like the Goddess?"

"Darker coloring—he's a true black—but they've both got the same big build and beautiful conformation."

"Who's training him? The same people who originally owned the filly?"

"Yup. D'Andrea Farm. Phil D'Andrea's the trainer."

They talked for a few minutes longer, then Ashleigh hurried back to the living room with her news. "That was Mike," she announced to Caroline, Linda, and Samantha.

"Like we didn't guess." Caroline laughed. "How'd he sound? Thrilled?"

"He could hardly talk. He'll be home tomorrow night. And there's more news," Ashleigh said quickly. "Fleet Goddess's half brother ran in a maiden race at Belmont today—and won."

"Really?" Samantha said excitedly. "Did Mike see him run?"

Ashleigh repeated what Mike had said.

"Hey, that's good news for you, Ash," Linda said. "Although siblings don't always show the same talent."

"Mike says he's coal black. So was Battlecry, and Charlie thinks the filly has the look of her sire, too."

"Enough of racing!" Caroline cried. "I thought you guys were going to show me the dresses you bought for the junior prom." As usual, Caroline had a one-track mind when it came to clothes.

"They're up in the bedroom," Ashleigh told her, but she was still thinking about Mike and the exciting news about the Goddess's half brother.

As soon as Linda left for home, Ashleigh rushed up to the stables to tell Charlie Mike's news.

"So her half brother's already running," the old trainer said, fingering his lip thoughtfully. "I would have liked to see him run. Mike says he's got the look of the filly?"

"Yes."

"Might be a good sign."

"Good sign or not—I don't know how I'm going

to go on training Fleet Goddess," Ashleigh muttered. "I'd like to strangle Brad."

"Pretty nifty, huh?" Corey asked Ashleigh and Mike as they all made their way into the high school gym the next Saturday night. The dimly lit gym was decorated with flower-covered trellises, and tables had been set up all around the perimeter. Along one wall was a table laden with drinks and snacks. And the band was set up at the opposite end of the gym. As chairman of the decorating committee, Corey had a right to be proud.

"You did an incredible job!" Ashleigh exclaimed. She glanced up at Mike and saw him smiling. He looked so handsome in his tux. She was pretty happy with her own appearance, too. The silky dress she'd chosen was soft and flowing, and Caroline had done Ashleigh's long, brown hair in a sophisticated twist.

"Hey, you guys. Over here!" They looked across the cloth-covered tables and saw Jennifer waving to them. As usual, she looked absolutely stunning, in ice blue. They all filed over—Corey and her current boyfriend, Peter Linder, Linda and her date, Brian McKinley, and Ashleigh and Mike. Jennifer had been talking about her date all week, though she wouldn't tell anyone who he was. Now she introduced them to a big blond guy, Tony DiMauro, who was one of the star freshman football players for the University of Kentucky. Jennifer was absolutely glowing as she made introductions.

"I've seen you around campus," Mike said as he and Tony shook hands.

"And I saw you on TV last week," Tony answered with a grin. "Nice horse you've got there—not that I'm an expert. I'm from outside Boston, and the only track up there just reopened."

"We have this whole table, don't we?" Corey asked. "Brenda and Larry are sitting with us, too. Are they here yet?"

While they sorted out the seating, the guys went off to get drinks. The gym was filling rapidly, and by the time Mike and the others returned with the drinks, the band had started their first set.

"The band sounds good," Mike said to Ashleigh. "Do you feel like dancing?"

Ashleigh looked out to the floor. Several couples were already out there. They wouldn't be the only ones dancing. She nodded.

Mike was a great dancer, and within seconds Ashleigh had relaxed. They stayed on the floor for two more dances—one slow, one fast—then returned flushed and breathless to the table.

"I think it's going to be a good prom," Linda leaned over to say to Ashleigh. "What do you think of Jennifer's date?"

"He's cute."

"Seems pretty nice, too, not like some of the other jerks she's fallen for."

"She had the hots for Mike a couple of years ago, remember," Ashleigh said with a twinkle.

"Mike's the exception," Linda said quickly.

Mike leaned toward them. "Did I hear my name mentioned?"

The next hours flew by. The band was incredible and the floor was packed for every dance. Ashleigh couldn't believe it when she looked at her watch and saw it was almost midnight.

"Whew!" Linda said to Ashleigh. "I'm wiped out! We're going back to your place for something to eat, aren't we?"

"Yup. My mother and I spent an hour this afternoon making sandwiches."

"Well, I'm ready for more food," Peter said. "The snacks here are all gone." Tony and Brian nodded their agreement.

"Okay," Corey said, taking over as social director as usual. "Let's get the show on the road."

A half hour later, a three-car caravan pulled up in front of the Griffens' house. The lights were on, and Ashleigh saw Justin's car parked in the driveway. She led everyone into the kitchen. She knew her parents would be in bed, since they had to be up at the crack of dawn, but her sister and Justin were in the kitchen. Caroline had already set out the huge tray of sandwiches.

"Hey, thanks," Ashleigh said.

"No prob. Justin and I just got back from the movies. Drinks are in the fridge," she said to the others.

"Help yourselves," Ashleigh added. "We've got ham, tuna, egg salad, and roast beef."

"Food!" Peter cried, grabbing two sandwiches

for himself. The others were right behind him.

"I want to see Wonder's Pride," Corey said when they'd finished the last of the sandwiches and were digging into a plate of home-made cookies. "Is it too late to go visit them?"

Ashleigh hadn't thought of going out to the barn, but she never missed an opportunity to show off Wonder and her foal. "Not if you're quiet," she said. "Most of the horses will be sleeping, and they'll get upset if there's a commotion."

"We'll be quiet as mice," Corey promised.

"Come on, then." Ashleigh led the way across the drive and quietly opened the barn door. A dim night-light lit the interior. A few horses snuffed and grunted, but the barn was pretty still. She walked quietly down the aisle to Wonder's stall and looked over the half door. The others followed, gathering behind her.

Wonder was lying on the bedding with her legs tucked beneath her. Wonder's Pride was curled up in a ball at her side. Both were peacefully asleep, but then Wonder's ears flicked forward, and she sleepily opened her eyes.

Before the mare could become alarmed, Ashleigh whispered, "It's just me and my friends, girl. Go back to sleep."

Wonder whuffed through her nose, then turned her head to check her foal. Although he'd grown a lot over the past two months, he still looked like a fuzzy ball. His oversize ears flicked back and forth as he began to wake up, and his small nostrils flared, sniffing the air. He lifted his head, shaking it sleepily as he focused on the watchers.

He looked up at them inquisitively, then pulled his long legs beneath him and pushed to his feet. He took a couple of wobbly, sleepy steps toward the stall door, his brush of a tail flicking behind him.

Wonder was instantly on her feet. She touched her foal gently with her nose and walked over to Ashleigh. She eyed the others as she thrust her head over the stall half door and rubbed the side of her head against Ashleigh's arm.

"Sorry, girl," Ashleigh said softly, scratching behind the filly's ears. "We didn't mean to wake you up."

"He's gorgeous," Corey whispered.

"So Wonder's the filly who won the Belmont, the Kentucky Derby, and Breeder's Cup," Tony murmured. "She acts like a pet."

"Yes, Wonder and I are good buddies, and we'd better go and let them get back to sleep before she gets mad at me." Ashleigh kissed Wonder's nose. "See you later, girl."

Wonder blew out a sweet-scented breath, and Ashleigh led her friends out of the barn.

"Is he going to be your next champion?" Tony asked as they walked back to the house.

"I hope he's going to be as good as his mother, but he's got a lot of growing up to do. He won't start training until he's nearly two. I've got another two-year-old filly I'm training now. Fleet Goddess."

111

"I'll remember the name," Tony said.

Mike stayed after the others left a few minutes later. He and Ashleigh went to sit and talk on the front porch.

"It was a really nice night," he said.

"I had a wonderful time," Ashleigh told him, laying her head on his shoulder. "And in just a few days school will be out. Oh, I didn't tell you! Mr. McLean talked to me today. He has to go north with his string in a week and asked if Sammy could stay with us while he's gone. My parents said it was fine, of course."

"What does Sammy think of it?"

"She thinks it's great. She's happy her father is going away for a while. She says he's been so depressed since her mother died that he could really use some time alone. I think she's also looking forward to spending time away from her father," Ashleigh added. "He tends to be overprotective of her."

"It'll be a perfect opportunity for you to get to know her better, too," Mike said. "That girl adores you, you know."

Ashleigh smiled. "Yeah, I hope I can somehow bring her out of her shell. She seems to have a lot bottled up inside her."

10

ON THE LAST DAY OF SCHOOL, ASHLEIGH AND LINDA flew out of the school doors and headed out to the parking lot.

"Summer at last!" Linda said. "Boy, am I ready. And I even pulled off a *B* in English!"

"I told you that you would. Corey got her *A* in chemistry. She looked pretty psyched."

"How did you do?" Linda asked.

Ashleigh passed over her final grades, and Linda skimmed them. "Honors again?"

"I didn't *always* do this well," Ashleigh reminded her.

"Yeah, I remember!"

"Oh, Linda, I wish you weren't going away again this summer."

"My father and I won't be going for another month, not until Saratoga opens," Linda said. "Maybe you could get Fleet Goddess ready to

113

run her maiden race up there!"

"I doubt if she's going to be ready," Ashleigh said. "Since Brad told me I can't use any of the exercise riders, I'm stuck. My parents don't want me touching much more of Wonder's winnings, so I don't think I can afford to hire a rider. I've been working her on the oval, but she still has a tendency to run out on the turns, and I don't know how she'll behave if I take her out on the trails alone."

"Now that school's out, maybe I can come over and ride with you," Linda offered. "Not tomorrow, though. I have to help my father work his horses, but maybe later this week."

"Great! I can use any help I can get," Ashleigh said eagerly.

Samantha wandered out behind the stable to the paddock where the exercise ponies, Belle and Dominator, were grazing in the sunlight. She was angry. What did she have to look forward to this summer? Being Fleet Goddess's groom was wonderful, but it would never be enough. She wanted to ride!

Leaning her arms on the top of the fence rail, she stared out at the horses. Dominator lifted his head, saw her at the fence, and ambled over. Samantha still had a carrot in her pocket, left over from the treats she'd given Fleet Goddess. She dug it out and fed it to the gelding, who eagerly chewed and bobbed his head in thanks.

As she patted Dominator's dark head, she had an idea. Why not? Her father had been the only obstacle to her riding—and he'd left that morning and wouldn't be back for at least a month. A niggling prick of conscience told her that what she was considering was wrong. Even though she hadn't talked to her father recently about riding, she didn't think he had changed his mind. In fact, she was almost certain he hadn't.

"But I'm sick of being treated like a baby," she muttered to herself. "If I leave it up to my father, I'll never ride again. Besides, Ashleigh needs my help."

Dominator grunted at her words, then nudged her with his nose, looking for another carrot.

"I'm going to do it," she said.

A moment later, she was striding purposefully back up to the stable in search of Ashleigh. Samantha found her outside Fleet Goddess's stall. "Do you still want to take Goddess out on the trails today?" she asked.

"I do," Ashleigh said with a frown, "but Linda can't come over until later in the week."

"I'll ride Dominator," Samantha said quickly, before she could change her mind.

Ashleigh stared at her. "But I thought—"

"It's okay."

"Are you sure?"

Samantha nodded firmly. Now that she'd made the decision, she was glad she had. She didn't let herself think ahead to the consequences if her father found out. She saw the flash of relief on Ashleigh's face.

"This is incredible," Ashleigh said. "And you

couldn't have better timing. Did you talk to your father last night?"

Samantha mumbled a response. She *had* talked to her father last night—just not about riding.

"Well, then let's go out right now," Ashleigh said excitedly. "Why don't you bring Dominator up, and I'll tack up Goddess."

Samantha grabbed a lead shank and hurried out to the paddock. She was going to ride again!

Dominator's ears pricked forward, and he whickered eagerly when he saw the lead shank in her hand. He knew what that meant. Samantha quickly opened the gate, clipped the shank to the gelding's halter, and led him out to the stable yard.

She saw Charlie sitting in his usual spot, watching all the activity around him. He looked up from the *Racing Form* he was studying and frowned when he saw her leading Dominator.

She hurried into the barn before he could question her. She had never deliberately disobeyed her father before. Until he had forbidden her to ride, there had never been any reason to.

Ashleigh had already brought out Dominator's saddle and bridle, and Samantha quickly tacked him up. In a moment the two girls had led the horses from the stable and were mounted. Samantha felt another quick jab of guilt, but it felt so wonderful to be in the saddle again! It had been more than a year since her mother had died. She thought of her mother, and felt tears spring to her eyes. But her mother wouldn't have wanted her to stop riding.

116

Her mother would have wanted Samantha to go on enjoying what she loved most to do.

"We'll take it easy this time out," Ashleigh said to Samantha. "You haven't ridden in a while, and you're going to be pretty sore if you do too much today. I just want Goddess to relax and have a good time. Okay?"

"Okay," Samantha said. They set off at an energetic walk up one of the grassy lanes between the paddocks.

When they'd reached the end of the first paddock fence, Ashleigh called over, "Let's trot them." Samantha nodded, and both horses stepped out eagerly.

Samantha couldn't stop the smile growing on her face as she and Ashleigh posted along to the rhythm of the horses' strides. She had missed riding, but she hadn't realized just how much until now. And it was all so familiar. She felt so at home on horseback, feeling the powerful strides of the horse and hearing the dull pound of hoofbeats on the grass.

They reached the top of the rise. Below them was a panoramic view of Townsend Acres—the freshly painted buildings, the green-grass paddocks, and the sleek animals inside them. They trotted on. Dominator seemed to be having as good a time as Samantha was, and he was perfectly behaved, responding to the slightest touch of the reins. Samantha glanced over at Fleet Goddess and saw the filly prancing along on elegant legs, relaxed and happy in the open air.

117

"There's a narrow section up here," Ashleigh called as they neared a dip in the trail. "We'd better walk them for a while." Fleet Goddess balked for a bit, but when she saw Dominator calmly walking beside her, she settled down.

Ashleigh looked over with a smile. "How're you doing?"

"Great!" Samantha breathed.

"You've got a good seat," Ashleigh said.

"Thanks."

"And Fleet Goddess is behaving well. You feel up to a short canter?" Ashleigh asked when they approached the long, straight galloping path that led back to the stable yard. Samantha nodded eagerly.

"You can relax with him," Ashleigh added. "He'd never try to bolt. And if the filly can see him alongside, it should help keep her in line."

Fleet Goddess snorted happily as they picked up the pace and swept along the flat half-mile stretch under the trees. Samantha sat back and reveled in feeling the wind in her face as the two Thoroughbreds matched strides. This was where she belonged!

All too soon Ashleigh was calling over to her to slow. They were nearing the stable yard. Reluctantly Samantha pulled Dominator back to a trot, but only when she saw the stable buildings ahead did her lighthearted mood begin to fade.

As they trotted down the last bit of lane, she saw two figures standing outside the trainers' office, watching. Her stomach instantly clenched in a knot. All she could think of was that her father had come back, and now she was going to get it.

She lifted her chin and straightened her shoulders defiantly, but as they drew closer, she saw that it wasn't her father. Mr. Townsend was talking with one of the grooms.

Samantha let out a breath of relief as she and Ashleigh crossed the stable yard at a walk, stopped the horses, and dismounted.

"I can't believe it," Ashleigh said, laughing. "Now I can start making real plans again. We'll give her a few more works on the trails before taking her back to the oval. We can go out in the mornings before it gets too hot. That sound good to you?"

"Sounds great." But at Ashleigh's enthusiasm Samantha felt another twinge of guilt. She noticed Charlie was scowling from his deck chair. The trainer rose and walked over to the girls.

"Good ride?" he asked Ashleigh.

"Perfect."

Samantha didn't dare look Charlie in the eye. She busied herself unsaddling Dominator. "I guess I'll take him back to the paddock," she said quickly. "He doesn't look like he needs to be cooled out."

"No, he doesn't," Ashleigh agreed.

Samantha clipped the shank to Dominator's halter and led him away.

When she was gone, Ashleigh turned to Charlie. "I'm so glad her father's let her ride again. It's going to make all the difference. She's got gentle hands and a good seat. You can tell she's had a lot of experience."

Charlie made a grunting noise in his throat.

"What's wrong?" Ashleigh asked in surprise. "I thought you'd be glad."

"Just seems a little strange that she waits till the day her father leaves to start riding again."

"She wouldn't disobey him," Ashleigh said.

Charlie scratched his neck. "You can't wrap a kid like her in cotton and expect her not to rebel. She's got too much energy and a mind of her own. McLean's been keeping her on a pretty short lead. Well, just keep it in mind. Since the doc won't let me ride yet, you need the help." With that Charlie shuffled off.

Would Samantha lie about having her father's permission? Ashleigh wondered. She shook her head. No, she just had a feeling Samantha was too honest to do that, even though secretly Ashleigh thought the girl had good reason to rebel.

11

"KEEP HER GOING LIKE THAT, AND WE'LL BE GETTING somewhere," Charlie said two weeks later as Ashleigh rode Fleet Goddess off the oval. Samantha followed right behind on Dominator. They'd just finished the filly's second gallop at a mile, and with Dominator galloping alongside, she was finally calming down and setting her mind to business.

"She's learning," Mike said with a grin. He'd given both Jazzman and Indigo a day off and had come over to watch the morning workouts. "She doesn't look quite as green anymore."

"She doesn't, does she?" Ashleigh beamed like a proud mother. "And she's raring to go. I still haven't let her out all the way."

"She's got a ways to go before you start breezing her," Charlie said.

"I know, but it doesn't hurt to plan ahead."

Charlie pulled off his battered hat and wiped a

red handkerchief across his brow. "Gonna be a hot one. They'll both need a good walk to cool them out."

Both girls had dismounted, and Ashleigh quickly checked over the filly, feeling her legs for any signs of heat, but the filly was in great shape and still had enough energy left to crane her head around and playfully nip the seat of Ashleigh's jeans.

"Hey!" Ashleigh cried, and stood up. "She's just full of herself today. She knows she did a good job out there, don't you, girl?" she asked, dropping a kiss on the filly's nose.

"Of course she's full of herself," Charlie grumbled. "The way you two spoil her."

"Oh, come on, Charlie," Ashleigh said. "Hank's told me how much time you spend at her stall."

The old trainer just shook his head and started back toward the stables.

"I think he's feeling more like himself again," Mike said, smiling.

"Thank heavens," Ashleigh said. She had driven Charlie to the doctor's that week for a checkup, and he'd come out of the doctor's office looking satisfied, though he was still on medication. Hank had told Ashleigh that Charlie had some sort of heart condition, so she was relieved to know he was improving. "I don't even care if he grouches at me all the time," she added, "as long as he gets better."

Samantha fit right into the Griffen household, and both Ashleigh's parents told her how much they liked the girl. "She's quiet," Mrs. Griffen said, "but I'm sure that has a lot to do with losing her mother. She's seemed a lot happier since she's started riding with you."

"She loves it," Ashleigh said. "She's a natural. I still get the feeling there's something's bothering her, though."

"It takes a long time to heal, Ash, but I'm glad you're being such a good friend to her."

"I forget sometimes that she's only thirteen. She doesn't act it."

"No." Mrs. Griffen smiled. "Especially when you compare her to Rory. They're about the same age, but she's much more mature."

Rory at that moment came bounding into the kitchen, dressed in his baseball uniform. He was playing shortstop on the summer community team and Ashleigh was giving him a ride to practice. "Okay, I'm ready!" he called. "I'll meet you in the car, Ash."

He whizzed through the room and out the back door, letting the screen slam shut behind him. "Thanks for giving him a ride, Ashleigh," Mrs. Griffen said. "I thought Sammy was going to ride into town with you two."

"She is. She went out to the paddock to see Wonder and Wonder's Pride. I thought I'd take her to the tack store. It's her favorite place in Lexington."

"Sounds like you at that age," Mrs. Griffen said, smiling. "Have fun."

Ashleigh went out to the paddock to get

Samantha. They both lingered for a moment, watching Wonder and the colt. He was almost three months old, and Ashleigh couldn't believe how much he'd grown. He'd nearly tripled in weight, though he was still awkward and gangly. Ashleigh felt her heart warm as she watched him romp around Wonder, who was keeping a patient, loving eye on him. "Beautiful, huh?" she said to Samantha.

Samantha smiled. "They are. It's really amazing to watch him grow."

After they had dropped Rory off at the ball field, Ashleigh and Samantha spent an hour in the huge tack store, walking up and down the aisles of saddles, bridles, boots, riding clothing, and other horse gear. Ashleigh loved the place, with its strong smell of good leather.

"Boy, it would be great to have a lot of money to spend in here," Samantha said longingly. "My mother and I used to buy all my father's tack for him. There was this great place in Florida where Mom and I loved to shop—" Suddenly Samantha stopped and bit her lip.

Ashleigh could see the tears welling up in the girl's eyes.

For a moment Samantha stood silently fighting back her tears, then she took a deep, shuddering breath. "It's just that sometimes I forget . . . I . . . I can't believe she's not here anymore. . . ." Samantha's lip started to quiver again. "I miss her . . ."

"I know," Ashleigh said gently. "It's got to be

awfully tough." She could see Samantha was embarrassed to lose her composure in the store. "Come on. Let's go for a drive, and we can stop at McDonald's on the way back."

Samantha nodded. Ashleigh put her arm around Samantha's shoulders as they went out to the car, then she drove in silence while Samantha pulled herself together. Maybe, Ashleigh thought, a good cry was exactly what Samantha needed. The girl seemed to keep everything to herself, pretending to be strong. But inside, she was probably a mess.

A few minutes later, Samantha wiped her eyes with the back of her hand. "Sorry," she said hoarsely.

"There's nothing to be sorry about," Ashleigh told her. "You need to cry."

"It doesn't help my father . . . I mean . . . he really was in bad shape after the accident. . . ."

"I don't think he expects you to be strong all the time."

"No, I guess not," Samantha said softly. "But it's been so hard. At least he's happier now, working at Townsend Acres."

"Are you happier, too?" Ashleigh asked.

Samantha nodded. "It's not like last year. I didn't want to go to school or anything. But I like Townsend Acres. It's like home . . . and there're you and Goddess and Wonder and Wonder's Pride. It's just sometimes I feel really bad . . . and I always miss my mother."

"I know you must," Ashleigh said sympathetically.

"But if you're ever feeling bad and want to talk about it, you can come to me."

"Thanks." Samantha's lips turned up in a weak but grateful smile.

"Let's stop and get something to eat," Ashleigh said. "My treat."

Linda called Ashleigh that night. "My dad's decided to leave next week," Linda said.

"Already?" Ashleigh cried. "I thought you weren't leaving for Saratoga until the end of July."

"My father wants to get the horses settled before the Saratoga meet begins. We have six horses racing this year."

"I'm going to miss you."

"But you'll be coming up. Fleet Goddess is doing great now. She's bound to be ready to race in August."

"Do you think so? I really want to enter her in her maiden race before the end of summer so that if she does well, I can enter her in a stakes race this fall. That'll be a good prep for her three-year-old season. But it's going to be lonely around here for the next couple of weeks. Mike's leaving, too, for Belmont."

Mike called a few minutes later. "I've got news for you," he said. "I just heard from a trainer friend in New York. Son of Battle raced in an allowance today and won."

"Again?" Ashleigh exclaimed. "So he really is a decent horse."

"Sounds like. He beat some good two-year-olds.

I'll see you tonight, but I just thought I'd pass on the news."

The news made Ashleigh even more determined than before. Fleet Goddess was really beginning to show progress, but the important thing wasn't getting Fleet Goddess into a race—it was having her do well in that race. Much more was on the line since Ashleigh was Goddess's sole owner and trainer. She had to prove to herself and the others that she knew what she was doing.

"Go!" Ashleigh cried as the training gate doors flew open a few mornings later. She kneaded her hands along Fleet Goddess's sleek neck and the filly shot forward. Dominator and Samantha were right beside them as they tore up the track. It had taken nearly a week of repeated practice to get the filly to break cleanly and smoothly from the gate, but the work was paying off. Fleet Goddess's ears were back, alert to Ashleigh's every command. Her mind was on business as they swept around the turn, with Dominator and Samantha beside them on the outside.

Ashleigh had the filly in a firm hold. She could feel the bundle of power beneath her and knew the filly had a lot more to give. "Easy, girl," Ashleigh murmured. "Wait until the far turn."

Dominator matched strides with them as they swept into the turn. Both horses' hooves churned up the harrowed track. Their huffed breaths and the rhythmic thud of their feet were the only sounds in the morning air.

"I'm letting her out," Ashleigh called over to Samantha. She saw Samantha's quick nod. They'd already decided on their strategy. Samantha would keep Dominator on a slight hold and let the filly move to the front. Ashleigh wanted to see how the filly would do running alone on the lead.

As soon as Fleet Goddess felt the extra rein, she thrust her head forward and instantly picked up the pace. Effortlessly they surged into the lead. Ashleigh was amazed at the filly's power, and she knew Fleet Goddess wasn't even beginning to tire.

Then suddenly the filly's ears flicked up. She dropped the bit and slowed her pace. Ashleigh was so taken by surprise that for an instant she didn't react. Dominator surged up again on their outside. Ashleigh saw him out of the corner of her eye, and so did the filly. Instantly Fleet Goddess picked up the pace and put her head and neck in front of the gelding. She galloped forward strongly until she put some distance between Dominator and herself. Then her ears pricked again and she slowed her strides. *What is going on?* Ashleigh thought frantically. As they entered the stretch she pushed her hands hard along the filly's neck. "Keep going!" she cried. "Don't back off now!"

They swept past the mile marker pole with Fleet Goddess still just a neck in front of Dominator. Ashleigh stood in the stirrups and began pulling the filly up. Fleet Goddess was tossing her head, obviously pleased with herself. Ashleigh shook her own head and frowned.

"What was going on?" Samantha asked as she rode up alongside. "She kept dropping the pace."

Ashleigh continued to frown. "I have an idea of what was happening, but let me talk to Charlie." She rode Fleet Goddess off the oval.

Charlie had pushed back his hat and had his arms folded across his chest. "She's waiting on horses," Charlie said when Ashleigh rode up. "As soon as she gets the lead, she loses interest and starts playing around."

"That's what I was afraid of," Ashleigh said, groaning.

"A lot of horses do it. They need to run at other horses or have a horse running at them to stay interested."

"How do you fix it? Try holding her off the pace?"

"I would, though she could get frustrated and lose all interest. Don't look so glum," Charlie added. "She did that mile in decent time without ever really putting out. The problem will be a fast closer, catching her by surprise. Don't worry. It's early yet."

But Ashleigh knew she had less than a month if she was going to have Fleet Goddess ready for a race by mid-August.

"I thought she would just roar away from Dominator," Samantha said to Ashleigh as they walked the horses back to the stable.

"So did I," Ashleigh said. "And she could have if she wanted to. She seemed to think she'd done a great job just staying in front. I'll bet if you and Dominator had pressured her harder, she would have just cranked out another gear. Though I don't know for sure. Let's try rating her behind Dominator tomorrow and see how that works."

They'd walked both horses and were sponging them down in the shade of one of the spreading trees when Mike came up the drive in his pickup. Ashleigh smiled. She hadn't expected to see Mike that morning. She'd thought he'd be busy taking care of last-minute things. He was leaving the next day for New York. "Hi there," she called happily.

Mike grinned as he walked over. "I thought you'd like to see this. It just came in the mail." He handed her a copy of the tentative Saratoga racing schedule. Ashleigh immediately put down her sponge and flipped it open.

"Have you looked at it yet?" she asked Mike.

"Yup. Some of the races may change, but check out the second and third weeks of the meet. There are a couple of good spots for maiden two-year-olds. Of course, you don't know what the fields will be like yet."

Ashleigh scanned the pages, nodding to herself every so often. Fleet Goddess had her nose over Ashleigh's shoulder. Suddenly she dropped her head and lipped the page. Ashleigh quickly pulled the schedule away from the horse's mouth, but the filly had already left a distinct wet mark on the page.

"I think she's just picked her own race," Ashleigh said, laughing. "Listen to this: 'August 10th, six furlongs, purse $24,000, fillies, two-year-olds, maiden special weights.'"

Charlie had walked up as she was reading. "Sounds like a perfect spot to me."

"But that's only three weeks away!" Ashleigh cried.

"Yup. Give you two something to work toward."

12

MIKE AND JAZZMAN WON THE SUBURBAN HANDICAP IN mid-July, which put them in the lead for the American Championship Racing Series. Yet it wasn't Jazzman's usual easy romp. He had his head in front as he went under the wire, but he came out of the race with a badly bruised foot, and Mike was forced to take him out of training for a while.

"It's a bummer," Mike told Ashleigh when he returned from New York the last week in July. "He won't be doing any racing in August—maybe not even in September, but it could have been worse. The foot will heal."

"Does this mean you're not going to Saratoga?" Ashleigh asked.

"No, I'm definitely going. I've still got Indigo, and my father wants to bring up a couple of horses. Jazzman wouldn't have been racing up there anyway. Besides"—Mike smiled—"I'm looking forward to us spending time in Saratoga together."

"Good, because so am I." Ashleigh put her arm through his as they sat on the front porch steps. "My mother's going to drive up with Samantha, Charlie, and me in the van."

"Why don't you let me bring Goddess up?" Mike offered. "I should have thought of it before. I know we'll have extra room, and it'll save you the hassle."

"Boy, that would be a lot easier. You're sure you have room? I've never driven the van, and my mother isn't exactly keen on it. She'd much rather drive up in one of our cars."

"We have room, don't worry," Mike assured her. "How's the filly's training going? Did you make much progress while I was gone?"

Ashleigh gave him a report.

"Now that Jazzman's out of training," Mike said, "I'll have time to come and watch some of her workouts."

Ashleigh smiled. "I'd like that."

The next morning Ashleigh and Fleet Goddess finished up an especially good morning workout, which thrilled Ashleigh since they had only another week before leaving for Saratoga. Ashleigh stayed to talk to Charlie as Samantha rode Dominator toward the stable yard.

"She's going to make a good exercise rider," Charlie said as he watched Samantha ride off. "Determined little thing, too. I just wonder what her father's going to say about her riding out on the oval."

"I thought about that," Ashleigh admitted. "It's not the same as riding the trails, but Sammy's never told me she wasn't supposed to."

"You think she would?" Charlie asked, raising his brows. "The kid's in heaven out there. She's not going to cut her own throat." Charlie grimaced after the departing girl and horse.

"I'm so glad you're coming to Saratoga with us," Ashleigh said. "I'd be a wreck if I had to do it alone, especially since I'm riding, too." As proud as Ashleigh was of Fleet Goddess's training, she knew she couldn't have done it without Charlie's help.

"The doc gave me my traveling papers, so I'll be there," Charlie said, though Ashleigh could see the twinkle of pleasure in his blue eyes. "Let's hope the filly stays on her toes this next week. You'll need to get a couple of good works into her." Suddenly Charlie scowled. "Well, look who's back."

Ashleigh looked toward the stable yard to see Mr. McLean striding purposefully toward Samantha as she rode Dominator across the yard. Even from a distance Ashleigh could tell the normally mild-mannered trainer was angry. She and Charlie watched as he caught up with his daughter.

"Samantha!" he shouted.

Samantha gasped when she saw her father, and her face paled. "Dad! What are you doing here? I didn't know you were coming back so soon."

"Obviously," Mr. McLean said angrily. "I trusted

134

you, and as soon as my back was turned, you disobeyed me!"

Samantha stared at him for a second, then lifted her chin defiantly. "I had to. I wanted to ride—and Ashleigh needed my help!"

Mr. McLean blew up. "What kind of an excuse is that? You knew you didn't have my permission to ride—and you've been out on the training oval— the *last* place I wanted you to be. You could have gotten hurt . . . or killed!"

"Dad, I'm a good rider! And nothing happened."

"I've talked to you nearly every night on the phone," Mr. McLean said, rushing on, "and you haven't said a *word* to me about riding. I find out now you've been riding almost since the day I left."

"Please, Dad," Samantha pleaded, "I had to help out—and you never would have given me permission to ride." Samantha's voice was rising. "What else was I supposed to do when you treat me like a baby."

It was the wrong thing to say. The color rose to Mr. McLean's face and his jaw clenched. "Don't you ever talk to me in that tone of voice! You've lied to me, and I find out about it by overhearing two of the farm's grooms gossiping at Saratoga."

"That's why you came back?" Samantha gasped.

"Yes—feeling like a complete fool! I couldn't believe it at first. I absolutely couldn't believe that *my* daughter would lie to me . . ." Now there was hurt in Mr. McLean's voice.

Samantha's face crumpled. "But it was important to me to ride! You don't understand at all!" she cried.

"I understand enough to know you could get hurt. No more riding! Is that clear?"

Samantha jumped down from Dominator's saddle and raced toward the stable. Her father took Dominator by the reins and stared after her.

"Oh, no," Ashleigh said, looking at Charlie. "You were right." She handed Fleet Goddess's reins to Charlie and rushed off after Samantha.

She saw no sign of the girl in the stable building, but as she hurried down the aisle, she heard muffled sobs coming from the direction of the tack room. When she looked into the dimly lit room, she saw Samantha huddled in a corner with her face buried in her hands, crying her heart out.

Ashleigh quickly crossed the room and knelt down to put her arm around Samantha's shoulders. Samantha stiffened and gulped back another sob. "You heard?"

"I'm sorry," Ashleigh said. "I feel like it's partly my fault."

Samantha bit her lips, trying to pull herself together. She squeezed her eyes shut for a second, then took a shuddering breath. "It's not. And *I'm* not sorry," she said. "I'd do it again. It was the only way I could get to ride. He would never have let me, and riding is so important to me. But he doesn't care!"

"Sammy, he's just afraid for you because of what happened to your mother."

Samantha's lips trembled. "It's awful enough for

136

me that she died. Does he have to stop me from doing the one thing I love?"

"He doesn't mean to hurt you. He just doesn't want anything to happen to you." Ashleigh hesitated. "And he's angry and upset because you didn't tell him."

A shadow of guilt crossed Samantha's face. "But it wouldn't have made any difference if I *had* told him. He still wouldn't have let me ride. And now what's going to happen to Goddess? That doesn't matter to him either."

"Sammy, he probably said things he didn't mean because he was upset." Ashleigh gave Samantha's shoulders a gentle squeeze. "It'll work out. Once your father knows what a great job you've been doing—"

"You don't know what my father's been like . . . ever since my mother died. . . ." Samantha drew in another shaky breath, then straightened her shoulders. Her green eyes were red rimmed, but it was obvious that she wasn't going to talk anymore. "I've got to walk Goddess," she said.

"Hank will take care of her," Ashleigh told her.

"No, it's my job," Samantha said firmly, and rose. Ashleigh let her go. She didn't have any other choice. *If only there was something I could do*, Ashleigh thought, rising to her feet. She went out into the barn aisle, deep in thought. She got no farther than the stable yard when she saw Charlie motioning to her. She followed him around the corner of the barn where they'd have some privacy.

"You talked to the girl?" Charlie asked. When Ashleigh nodded, he added, "Figured I'd better talk to McLean. He was as upset as the girl. I don't think he realizes what a tight rein he's been keeping her on. Kept saying to me, 'I love her. I'm just trying to do what's best for her.'" Charlie rubbed his chin. "Told him that if he loved her, he had to let the kid go and be herself. You don't keep a fine racehorse locked in a stall and never let it take its chances on the track."

Ashleigh sighed. "I'm glad you talked to him. Did you tell him what a good rider she is and how much help she's been?"

"I told him he had reason to be proud of her riding. Don't know if it will do any good, but I reckon he'll be doing some thinking. Too bad—too bad all around."

That night Samantha moved her things back to her father's apartment. Ashleigh stopped her and asked worriedly, "Has your father said anything else?"

Samantha shook her head. "He's been out in the stable all day. All I know is that I have to stay inside tonight and probably for the rest of the week for lying." She hesitated. "I guess I really messed things up for you, too. What are you going to do about training Fleet Goddess?"

"I'll work something out. I think she's gotten to the point where working her on her own is enough."

"I hope so," Samantha said mournfully. "But I'm still glad I did it. If I never get to ride again, at least

I can remember the good time I had this summer." With that she ran off, her red hair billowing in a silky cloud behind her.

Ashleigh gave Fleet Goddess two good works early in the week while Samantha watched from the rail. She didn't whine or complain, but she looked miserable. And so did her father. When Ashleigh saw him at the oval, his face was drawn and he seemed lost in thought, but at least he hadn't forbidden Samantha to continue being Fleet Goddess's groom and to go to Saratoga.

The filly knew something was different when Ashleigh rode her out on the oval. She craned her head from side to side and snorted uneasily when she didn't see Dominator. Ashleigh soothed her and finally got her to settle down, but the filly didn't like the change in the routine.

Ashleigh knew that the filly's clocking wasn't great before she rode off the track and saw the pucker of Charlie's mouth. The only time Fleet Goddess had picked up the pace at all was when she'd caught a glimpse of one of Ian McLean's horses breezing in front of them.

"It's not as bad as you think," Charlie told her as she dismounted and gave a sigh of disgust. "She's going to have competition in the race, and once she eyeballs those horses running with her, she'll wake up and go after them."

Ashleigh wasn't so sure, but Mike agreed with Charlie. "Really, Ash, I can't see her slogging along like she did today—not considering what I've seen her do in the past."

"I hope you're both right," Ashleigh said, feeling doubtful about their chances in the race.

13

ON AUGUST 10 MIKE AND ASHLEIGH WALKED ALONG THE
line of stabling barns on the tree-shaded Saratoga
backside, trying to fill the hours before Fleet Goddess's first race. In the five days that they'd been at
Saratoga, Fleet Goddess had had a chance to settle
in and put in two works on the track, but as usual
Ashleigh was getting a severe case of prerace jitters.

"I think Goddess is getting used to the crowds
now," Ashleigh said, "and Sammy spends every
second she can with her."

"That's the only time I see a smile on her face,"
Mike remarked somberly. "I guess McLean hasn't
relented any in the last week."

"No—not that Sammy talks about it. She's
holding everything inside again." Ashleigh shook
her head. "But she loves the filly. She'll be as
bummed out as I will if we don't do well."

"Even if Goddess doesn't do as well as you

want, there's no reason to feel bad. It's her first race—a whole new experience for her."

"Brad will have something to say," Ashleigh said. "I've bumped into him a couple of times, and he practically sneers at me."

"Since when did you care what Brad thought?" Mike asked. "He's probably just jealous. None of the horses he brought up here this summer has done anything worth mentioning. The filly will learn from the race no matter what happens, and she's not going to make a jerk out of you. Relax."

Ashleigh laughed. "Some kind of advice coming from you. You're an absolute basket case when your horses race!"

"Yeah, I know," Mike said with a grin. "I guess it goes with the territory."

"What time is it?" Ashleigh had left her own watch at the motel. Mike cocked his wrist so she could read his. "Time to get back," she said with a little quiver in her voice. Not only did she have to make sure the filly was ready, but she had to change into jockey's silks—her very own silks in her chosen colors of maroon and silver. She prayed they'd bring her good luck.

"Charlie's there," Mike said. "He and Sammy will get the filly up to the receiving barn and to the walking ring. All you're going to have to do is ride her—and you *know* you can do that."

An hour and forty minutes later, Ashleigh filed into the tree-shaded Saratoga walking ring with the

142

rest of the jockeys riding in the fourth race. The crowd was six deep along the walking ring rail, but Saratoga always drew huge crowds during the summer, even in midweek.

Ashleigh clenched and unclenched her hands, trying to loosen up. Then she felt a tap on her shoulder and heard Craig Avery's voice. "You're going to do fine. Jilly's rooting for you. She just called me from California."

Ashleigh turned and smiled at Jilly's boyfriend. "So she's thinking of us all the way out at Del Mar! Tell her I said thanks. Goddess and I will try to give you a run for your money."

Craig grinned. "Don't tell the owners I said this, but the nag I'm on, Summary, is just that. You shouldn't have any problems beating us." He gave Ashleigh a wink as the jockeys separated and headed toward their mounts. Ashleigh saw her cheering squad standing near the rail of the walking ring—her mother, Mike, and Linda. They gave her big, encouraging smiles.

Even though Ashleigh was officially listed as Fleet Goddess's trainer, Charlie had filled in as her assistant and tacked up the filly moments before. He wore his usual prerace scowl as he stood beside the filly and Samantha. Samantha held the lead shank clipped to Fleet Goddess's bridle. The girl's face glowed with happiness.

"She's set and raring to go," Charlie said when Ashleigh had crossed the walking ring to stand beside them.

"I should try to get her out fast," Ashleigh said, as much to herself as Charlie.

"I would, with her in the first post position. Don't want to get squeezed or boxed in. Track doesn't seem to be showing much bias, so there's no advantage or disadvantage to running on the rail, except saving ground. If she doesn't come out fast and you find yourself boxed, try to pull her back and come around. I heard the four horse is a strong closer. Not much room for closers in a six-furlong race, but if she makes the lead, keep her on her toes. Don't let her get caught playing around, or you could lose it at the wire."

Ashleigh nodded. She hated whips, but she was carrying one today. She didn't intend to use it unless it was absolutely necessary, but if Fleet Goddess started waiting on horses, one quick flick might be the only way to get her attention. That is, Ashleigh thought, if they even made the lead.

The call came for riders to mount, and Charlie gave her a leg into the saddle. Samantha looked up. Her face was tense but excited. She gave Ashleigh a slightly quivering smile. "Good luck! I know she can do it."

Ashleigh smiled in return as she fastened the chin strap of her helmet and collected the reins. She smoothed her hand down the filly's neck. "There's going to be a big, noisy crowd out there," she said softly. "Just take it easy and don't let them bother you."

Fleet Goddess snorted in surprise as the escort rider led them onto the track and she caught sight and sound of the spectators in the packed grandstand. The noise was pretty deafening, and the filly fidgeted beneath her, but Ashleigh was sure most of the other maiden two-year-olds in the race would be fidgeting, too. At least the field would be breaking from the gate at the beginning of the backstretch—as far from the stands as they could get.

She tried to steady her own nerves and continued soothing the filly as they filed by the stands in the post parade. Then they started their warm-up jog to the gate. The first race was always the hardest for a horse, and the important thing was to do her best for Fleet Goddess so that the experience was a good one.

They loaded first. Fleet Goddess went in calmly, though she was still a little nervous, huffing as they waited for the rest of the field to load.

Ashleigh gently rubbed the filly's neck, then collected a rein and a fistful of Fleet Goddess's mane in each hand. She readied herself in the saddle, head up, eyes staring between Fleet Goddess's ears. The filly flicked them in anticipation. The last horse had loaded. There was a second's tense silence, broken only by the snorted breaths of the horses. Then the gate doors snapped open to ringing bells. "Go!" Ashleigh shouted.

Fleet Goddess leaped forward. So did seven other maiden fillies in a roar of pounding hooves. From their inside post position, Ashleigh could see only a small portion of the field as they jostled for position. Fleet Goddess easily put away the two fillies outside of them, but as the field thundered up the backstretch, another filly broke free from the middle of the pack to take the lead. Her jockey quickly angled her over to the rail in front of Fleet Goddess. A second filly followed suit. Fleet Goddess didn't like it one bit and started surging up on her own.

"Easy," Ashleigh told the filly as she took a firmer grip on the reins. There wasn't room to squeeze between the horses. They'd have to wait for a hole to open or go around the leaders. In a six-furlong race, there wouldn't be a lot of time to think about the next move, but they were only into the first quarter mile.

She glanced under her arm behind her. The leaders, with Fleet Goddess hot on their heels, were pulling away from the rest of the pack. The fourth runner was a good two lengths back. Ashleigh made a snap decision. She checked Fleet Goddess to get her attention, then tightened her right rein. The filly needed no further encouragement. She angled out toward the center of the track. Ashleigh straightened her, and they had a clear path up outside of the leaders.

Fleet Goddess immediately fought for more rein and started lengthening her stride, but it was too soon to go for the lead. Ashleigh didn't intend to make a move until they hit the quarter pole. But it wasn't easy holding the filly back. Ashleigh could feel the strain in her arms and hands as the filly dragged on the reins. They swept into the turn. The leaders had been setting fast fractions—Ashleigh could feel it—and those fast fractions would help a late closer, who would rush past tiring horses in the stretch.

She glanced back again, looking for the four horse, but no one was gaining outside of them. *Patience . . . patience*, she told herself as they came past the quarter pole, off the turn. Two furlongs, a quarter of a mile, to go. The leaders were tiring. Fleet Goddess was gaining on them without any urging from Ashleigh, but Ashleigh knew she couldn't hold Fleet Goddess on a tight rein much longer without frustrating the filly. And now she could hear rapidly approaching hoofbeats. A quick glance back told her the rest of the field was gaining on them. She let the filly out. Ashleigh could almost feel Fleet Goddess's shudder of delight. In two strides she charged past the leaders and pulled herself a length into the lead. The filly was roaring and still had tons of power in reserve.

They were at the sixteenth pole and in the lead by a length and a half. Ashleigh glanced back under her right arm. No horse was tearing up on their outside. *We're going to win it!* Ashleigh thought joyously. No sooner had the words flashed through her mind than Fleet Goddess pricked her ears and dropped off the bit.

"No!" Ashleigh cried to the horse. "Keep going! You haven't won yet!"

Neither of them saw the horse who had slipped through a narrow opening on the rail until it was abreast of Fleet Goddess. From the corner of her eye, Ashleigh saw the fast-closing blur come up neck and neck with them three paths in. She lifted her whip, but Fleet Goddess had seen the offender, too, and suddenly flattened her ears and leaped forward. But it was too late! The inside horse caught them by a nose at the wire.

Ashleigh groaned as she stood up in her stirrups, but Fleet Goddess refused to slow her stride until she was ahead of the winning horse once again. Only then did she break from her gallop and drop back into a canter.

Ashleigh let out a long breath. They'd come so close! If only Fleet Goddess hadn't started playing games. If only she'd been more prepared herself. She should have flicked the whip by Fleet Goddess's eye as soon as the filly slacked off the pace, but she couldn't be angry with the horse. She'd run a good race overall, and if she'd seen the horse on the rail in time, she probably would have won.

The others were all waiting as Ashleigh rode Fleet Goddess off the track. "A bad break," Ashleigh's mother said sympathetically. Samantha went to the filly's head. Ashleigh could see she was having trouble hiding her disappointment, but she lovingly patted the filly as Ashleigh dismounted. Fleet Goddess barely seemed winded, and she was prancing around, acting like she'd won the race. Maybe she thought she had.

"Not a bad race, all in all," Charlie said.

Ashleigh unfastened the girth and began sliding

the lightweight saddle off Fleet Goddess's back. "But she blew it when she got the lead. I blew it, too," she added. "I never thought to look inside. I didn't think a hole would open."

"Neither did I, but you've always got to be prepared," Charlie said. "It was a good learning experience."

"She came back when she saw the other horse," Mike said encouragingly. "She only lost by a nose."

"I know. She was trying," Ashleigh agreed.

"She can only improve off this race, Ash," Linda said. "She's got the ability. She was never even in top gear, and she looks like she could go around again without working up a sweat."

Ashleigh looked over at the filly and smiled. "You will learn from this, won't you, girl?" Fleet Goddess craned her neck around and blew out a soft breath.

"I thought so," Ashleigh said.

When Ashleigh had changed from her silks and returned to the backside, she was beginning to feel a little less disappointed. It hadn't hurt that a couple of the jockeys had told her that she had a decent little filly. Craig Avery had been especially impressed. "I'll be calling Jilly with the news tonight," he said.

After checking over Fleet Goddess, Ashleigh sat on a bench with Mike and Linda outside the filly's stall and gulped down a soda. Several people stopped by to talk about the race, including Frank Newton, a well-known New York trainer.

"Saw the race. Not interested in selling the filly, are you?" he asked.

"No," Ashleigh said, looking up at him in surprise.

"Too bad. I like the look of her. Decent first race, though she's got some quirks to iron out. Training her yourself?"

"Basically. Charlie Burke's been helping me."

"You can always tell when Charlie's had a hand in things. I'll give you a hundred thousand for her, on the spot."

Ashleigh nearly choked on her soda.

"I'm serious. I'll give you a certified check right now."

Linda was jabbing Ashleigh so hard with her elbow, Ashleigh had to give her friend a warning look. "I-I'm not interested," Ashleigh managed to stutter.

"That's more than a fair offer," the trainer argued.

Ashleigh shook her head. "She's not for sale."

"Well, if you change you mind, let me know. My office is just down the shed row." The trainer walked off.

"My God . . ." Linda sputtered. "Ash . . . a hundred thousand! He was serious."

Ashleigh was staring at the departing trainer with wide eyes.

"I guess that tells you something about the filly," Mike said with a grin.

"He *was* serious, wasn't he?" Ashleigh gasped.

Linda laughed. "Boy, have you got a reason to

get her ready for her next race now. Wait till Charlie hears."

Not surprisingly, Charlie just made a grunting noise when Ashleigh told him about the offer. "Glad you had the sense to refuse. If Frank Newton offers you a hundred, then the filly's got to be worth more."

"But I didn't even pay ten thousand for her!"

"Oh, thinking of selling her, are you?"

"No, of course not! But I was just surprised he offered so much."

"Word's getting around about her half brother," Charlie said. "He wins his next couple of races and people will start getting real excited."

Samantha burst in. "You're not going to sell Goddess, are you?" she gasped.

"Never—but it's kind of nice to know someone would pay that much for her."

14

BY THE TIME THEY RETURNED HOME FROM SARATOGA A few days later, Ashleigh was convinced that Fleet Goddess deserved a crack at a fall stakes race, and there was a good one at Keeneland in October. Ashleigh gave Fleet Goddess an extra day's rest, then started working her on the oval again.

Both Linda and Mike came over when they could to ride Dominator, though Jazzman was on the mend and Mike was gradually starting him back in training and getting him ready for the Jockey Club Gold Cup. The hard part was seeing the pain in Samantha's face when she watched Linda get into Dominator's saddle. Ashleigh wished there were something she could do, but she was afraid to pressure Mr. McLean. And he was bound to relent on his own sometime. He must have noticed how miserable his daughter was. He couldn't let her go on like that forever.

School would be starting again in just over a week, and Ashleigh wasn't entirely happy about that. She liked school, but she was so wrapped up in Fleet Goddess's training that she hated to spend any time away from her.

"I've got to get my act together about college," Linda said the week before Labor Day. "At least you've pretty much decided on the University of Kentucky so you can stay close to the farm."

"And Mike," Ashleigh said with a smile. "Yeah, I've pretty much decided. It's got the courses I want."

Linda wrinkled her nose. "I can't even decide what I want to study. My dad wants me to stay in the horse business, but Ash, I don't know. I love horses, but I know how much it ties you down. My parents can't go anywhere unless they hire someone to take care of the horses, and even then they worry all the time."

"You've got six months," Ashleigh reassured her, "and you can always do liberal arts or business until you decide."

"Right. That's true."

At dinner that night Ashleigh noticed her parents were acting a little strange—nervous, but excited, too. Caroline was leaving the next day for college in Louisville and had wanted to skip dinner to pack, but Mr. Griffen had practically ordered her to the table.

"What's the big deal about my missing dinner?" Caroline protested. "I can eat when I'm done packing."

"We have something important to tell all of you," he said.

Ashleigh frowned. What could be so important that they were practically holding a family conference?

"You know," Mr. Griffen said, "that we've always wanted to buy another breeding farm, ever since we lost our old farm, Edgardale, after that equine virus."

Ashleigh braced herself. She could tell that this was going to be big.

"Well, we've found one," her father continued with a smile. "We've been looking for a long time, and we finally found a place we both love. The facilities are wonderful, and the price is right. We put a deposit on it today."

For an instant there was dead silence at the table.

Finally Caroline spoke up. "But we didn't even know you were looking. Why didn't you tell us?"

"We weren't sure we could find anything we could afford—then this place came on the market out of the blue. I know we should have given you all some forewarning, but you'll like it. There's a wonderful farmhouse, barns, and a hundred acres of mostly pasture."

"Another farm? Where is it?" Rory demanded.

Ashleigh stared at her parents, frozen.

"On the other side of Lexington. The bank's already approved the mortgage. We should be able to move in less than a month. We've already talked to Clay Townsend, and he's advertising for new breeding managers."

154

Ashleigh finally found her voice, though it came out like a croak. "Leaving Townsend Acres? In less than a month?"

"Ashleigh," Mrs. Griffen said, "I know how much you love it here, but it's not as if we're moving that far away—only to the other side of Lexington. You can come back to visit anytime you like."

Ashleigh looked down at the table. What about Wonder and Wonder's Pride? She'd have to leave them. When Mr. Townsend had given her half ownership of Wonder, his one condition had been that Wonder would stay at Townsend Acres. And what about Charlie and Samantha and all her other friends—and Fleet Goddess?

"You know how we've dreamed of having our own place again, and we could never do better than this," Mrs. Griffen said enthusiastically. "It has everything—the land, the buildings, and even some very good breeding stock. The Townsends have been good to us, but it's not the same as being on our own farm—actually owning the stock that we're breeding and selling."

Ashleigh could understand her parents' feelings. She knew what it was like not to own the animal you cared for and loved. But all she could think of was what she would lose.

"After dinner we want to take you three over to see it," Mr. Griffen said. "You'll like it. We know you will."

For the rest of the meal Ashleigh toyed with the

155

food on her plate. She heard the others talking, but the words wouldn't penetrate her brain. How could her parents do this to her? Especially now, when she had Fleet Goddess in intensive training—and they hadn't said anything about training facilities at the new place. She had so many dreams for Wonder's Pride, too. She'd wanted to take part in his training when he was ready, and Mr. Townsend would have let her. But if she didn't live here—

Ashleigh and her family pulled into the drive of their new property an hour later. Fenced paddocks spread out on either side of the drive. At the end was a brick farmhouse, older than the one they were living in, but neat and cozy. Behind it were two barns and several outbuildings, then more acres of gently rolling green pastures. It was pretty. Ashleigh had to admit that, even though she hated to.

Caroline and Rory toured the house, growing more and more excited about moving. Downstairs there was a big country kitchen, a dining room, and a living room with a fireplace. Upstairs were three big bedrooms, two bathrooms, and a smaller room that her parents could use as an office.

"Hey, this is twice as big as my old room!" Rory exclaimed. "Yeah, I like this place!"

Ashleigh saw her parents exchange a glowing look of happiness, and she knew she couldn't tell them how devastated *she* felt. The place was perfect for them. The barns were immaculate and up-to-date, the pastures were in good condition, and the stock that filled the stalls and grazed in the pastures were fine examples of Thoroughbreds. But as Ashleigh had guessed, there were no training facilities on the farm. She couldn't bring Fleet Goddess here and keep the filly in training, and she already had to leave Wonder and Wonder's Pride behind!

Her mother saw the fallen expression on her face. "We know it's a disappointment to you not to have a place to train," she said, "but I'm sure you can keep Goddess at Townsend Acres. We could make some kind of arrangement with Clay Townsend."

Ashleigh nodded numbly.

She called Mike as soon as she got home. Caro left the bedroom, so Ashleigh could talk in privacy. "I had no idea your parents were thinking of buying another farm," Mike said, stunned.

"Neither did I," Ashleigh told him.

"I can't believe it."

"The new place is nearly twenty miles from here," Ashleigh said. "That means I'll have to get up at three to make it over here to work the filly and still have time to get to school. And it will probably mean I'll have to stop helping Charlie with his horses."

"You can always bring the filly over here and use our track," Mike said, "but that's not going to help you timewise. You'll still have a long drive back and forth before school, and Charlie would sure miss having the filly around. I can tell he's getting excited about her."

"And Samantha would be *really* upset if I moved Goddess."

"Have you told her yet?"

157

"No. We just got back from looking at the new place. I'll talk to everyone in the stables in the morning."

"I'll come over as soon as I'm done working the horses," Mike promised.

Next Ashleigh dialed Linda. "You're going to move?" Linda cried into the receiver. "Oh, no! That's awful, Ash! I can't believe it, though I know your parents have always wanted their own farm."

"I guess I shouldn't be so selfish."

"I don't think you're being selfish!" Linda exclaimed. "I'd be totally freaked if I were you. But at least you won't be changing schools."

Caroline came into the bedroom as Ashleigh and Linda were talking. When Ashleigh hung up, she sat down on the bed. "Ash, it won't be as bad as you think. I know how you feel about this place, but you'll be able to come back whenever you want. Mr. Townsend isn't going to stop you from seeing Wonder. She's half yours."

Ashleigh rubbed a hand over her eyes. "I know," she said with a sigh. "It's just going to be so different . . . and there's Fleet Goddess, too."

"You'll work something out. Give it a couple of days, and you'll feel better."

Ashleigh nodded, but she doubted she would.

The next morning she broke the news to Charlie, Hank, and Samantha. Charlie's mouth tightened. "Thought there was something in the wind. There's been a rumor flying around here that Townsend was looking for new breeding managers. Didn't want to believe it."

"You can't move!" Samantha cried. The girl's face was absolutely white, and Ashleigh could almost read her thoughts—Samantha was finally starting to feel at home, and Ashleigh was her closest ally. If Ashleigh left, she'd be alone again.

"We won't be moving for nearly a month," Ashleigh said quickly, trying to reassure her, "and I'll be coming over all the time to see Wonder and Wonder's Pride."

"What about Goddess?" Samantha asked nervously.

"I'm going to arrange with Mr. Townsend for her to stay here. There aren't any training facilities at the place my parents are buying."

Samantha looked a little less devastated, but later that morning Ashleigh found her leaning on the rails of Wonder's paddock, staring out at the mare and foal.

Ashleigh leaned her arms on the rail next to Samantha and spoke quietly. "I know. I'm feeling pretty bad myself."

"What am I going to do if you move away? You're my only friend."

"You must have made some friends at school," Ashleigh said.

"Yeah, a couple, but none of them are as interested in horses as I am. I mean, they ride and stuff, but they're not really serious."

Ashleigh understood. She'd sometimes felt the

same way when she was Samantha's age, except that she'd had Linda, who was as nuts about horses as she was.

"And if you go away, I'll *never* get to ride again."

"What do you mean?" Ashleigh asked.

"My father might change his mind if I ride with you, but he'll never let me if I'm alone. He'll be too afraid something will happen." Samantha tightened her jaw angrily. "I'll run away."

"No, you won't," Ashleigh said quickly. "That wouldn't help."

Samantha dropped her chin onto her folded arms. "I guess I don't mean it. It's just been so crummy since my father stopped me from riding! If I didn't have Goddess to groom, I really *would* run away."

"Well, Goddess isn't going anywhere, and neither are Wonder and the foal," Ashleigh said. "I'm going to be counting on you to keep an eye on them for me. And don't worry. I'm sure your father will change his mind about letting you ride."

Samantha didn't look convinced.

Wonder had lifted her head from grazing and had seen Ashleigh and Samantha talking. She trotted over with her rapidly growing foal in her wake. His head was as high as Wonder's shoulder, and although he still seemed out of proportion, he had filled out even more, and his coat had lost most of its fuzzy look. He bounded away from the other mares and foals, kicking up his heels playfully as he followed Wonder.

Ashleigh pulled out some carrots and fed one to Wonder as she scratched the mare's ears. Wonder's Pride nosed in curiously, trying to get his head over the paddock rail. A few days before, Mr. Townsend had sent in the registration papers for the foal and had officially named him Wonder's Pride. At least Ashleigh didn't have to worry about Wonder's Pride going to auction. Mr. Townsend was too impressed with the foal to consider selling him. In another year he would go into training and hopefully become a member of the farm's next generation of stars.

"It's going to be weaning time next month," Ashleigh said to Samantha, hoping to snap her out of her blue mood. "You've never been around a farm for weaning, have you?"

Samantha shook her head. "I've never been on any breeding farm until now."

"It's a hard time for the horses. All the mares and foals are separated—the mares go into one paddock, the foals into another."

"Do they have to do it that way—so suddenly?"

"It's easier in the long run, but I'll be here with them," Ashleigh said, "even if the new breeding managers have taken over."

15

THAT WEEKEND ASHLEIGH WAS RIDING FOR CHARLIE IN A small race at nearby Turfway. Charlie was sending one of his claimers over in the van with a couple of Maddock's horses. Ashleigh wondered if Charlie had asked her to ride just to take her mind off her move, but as Ashleigh prepared for the race, she realized she was glad for the change of scene. She'd invited Samantha to come along, and Mr. McLean had agreed to let her go since they'd be gone only for the day.

"Big field," Charlie told Ashleigh once she was mounted, "but I think we've got a chance. These aren't the best horses. You know this guy likes to run off the pace, so just let him settle and find a spot four or five back. Start moving him at the quarter pole and that should get you in good position for the stretch drive."

"All set," Ashleigh said.

"Good luck!" Samantha called.

Ashleigh put her mind on the race ahead as the field moved through the post parade and warm-up. They were in the number-six slot. Ashleigh got the horse out cleanly, but they'd only gone a stride or two when the number-seven horse veered over and bumped them. Quickly Ashleigh checked and steadied her mount, but they'd lost a couple of strides on the field. They were close to last when Ashleigh had the horse moving smoothly again and started weaving him through the stragglers at the back of the pack, trying to work forward to sit four or five horses off the leaders.

Her mount was ready and eager, and without much effort, they started picking off horses. As they came off the clubhouse turn, they were up into seventh in the fourteen-horse field. Then they squeezed between two horses, up into fifth. Two lengths ahead of them, three horses were running abreast across the track. Ashleigh waited for an opening. They were only halfway down the backstretch, and she still had time. She was sure the outside horse was tiring and would soon drop back, giving her room to go around the other two and attack the leader.

She readied herself for the move. Then suddenly the horse in front of her went down! Its jockey flew over its head onto the dirt track. The jockeys to either side of the fallen horse frantically maneuvered to stay clear of the downed jockey. Ashleigh checked her own mount hard, hauling on the reins, trying to go clear of the fallen animal, but they were too close. Her mount suddenly lifted into the air, trying to leap over the fallen horse. Ashleigh thought they would make it, but the animal was off balance. They, too, were suddenly going down in a tangle! Ashleigh was jettisoned out of the saddle, over the horse's head. She flipped in midair and landed hard on her upper back and neck. In a daze she heard the thundering pound of hooves as the rest of the field passed by to either side of her. She tried to lift herself up on her elbows, but stopped when she felt the sharp pain in her back. She turned her head, trying to see if her mount was up on his feet, but both fallen horses were out of her line of vision. The next thing she knew, the other jockey was leaning over her.

"You okay?"

"I don't know," she whispered. "My back hurts."

"Don't move a muscle till the ambulance gets here."

"My mount?" she asked.

"Up, but he's favoring his right fore."

"Your horse?" she asked.

He shook his head.

Ashleigh closed her eyes. She hated track accidents. She hated to know an animal had been injured. When she opened her eyes, the ambulance crew had arrived and was checking her over and asking her questions. They slipped a support board beneath her, strapped her to it, and carried her to the ambulance.

"Charlie . . . Sammy . . ." she muttered, but the attendant hushed her. Then all she heard was the ambulance siren as she was rushed off the track to the nearest hospital. She felt helpless and alone as she was shuffled through exams and X rays. As she was wheeled to a room for a few minutes peace, she saw Charlie and Samantha coming up the brightly lit hallway. Charlie had his hat in his hands and had crushed it into an unrecognizable shape. Samantha's face was deathly pale. Ashleigh thought for a moment that the girl was going to faint, but Charlie had an arm around her shoulders to brace her.

A nurse stopped Charlie and spoke to him as Ashleigh was being wheeled into the room. A moment later he joined Samantha and Ashleigh in the room.

"Scared the daylights out of me," Charlie said, coming to the side of the bed with Samantha. "Maddock has put a call through to your parents."

"How's the horse?" Ashleigh asked.

Charlie pursed his lips and sighed. "We'll have to put him down. Broke his right cannon bone. Injury's too severe to try and save him."

Tears flooded Ashleigh's eyes. "Oh, no! He tried to get over the other horse. I—I tried to get him clear . . . but there was nowhere to go. Oh, God, it's my fault. I should have reacted faster."

"There wasn't a thing you could have done. You didn't have room to maneuver." Charlie shook his head. "Hate accidents like this, but they happen, and in this case, no one's to blame."

Samantha still hadn't said a word, but she'd started to tremble like a leaf in the wind. Charlie grabbed a chair and made her sit down, just as one of the doctors who had examined Ashleigh came in. He held a sheaf of X rays in his hand. He and Charlie introduced themselves to each other.

"Well, the good news is that you haven't broken anything," the doctor said cheerfully. "But you've definitely traumatized your neck. We're going to fit you with a neck brace. I want you to stay reasonably quiet for the next week. It goes without saying—no riding until the brace comes off, and I recommend the brace stay on for at least a month. I'll be giving your parents your X rays, but you'll need to continue seeing a specialist in Lexington. You're a lucky young lady, you know. You could easily have broken your neck."

Ashleigh didn't feel very lucky at the moment. Each of the doctor's words settled like a lead weight. She hadn't had time to think ahead—until now. Fleet Goddess was racing in a month; they were moving in less time than that; school was starting that Tuesday. And she was out of commission. How was she going to train Fleet Goddess? Who was going to ride her?

Ashleigh was released from the hospital when her parents arrived. They were upset and worried, but relieved to see that Ashleigh was awake and alert. Mr. Griffen and Charlie picked up her car at the track and drove it home while Mrs. Griffen drove Ashleigh and Samantha in the family car. It was a long and uncomfortable drive home, but Ashleigh didn't complain. She was feeling so down, her physical aches didn't seem to matter. It was late by the time they got back to the farm, and Mrs. Griffen made up the bed in the den and ushered Ashleigh straight into it. Rory looked in with a worried face, but Mrs. Griffen shooed him away. "You can talk to Ashleigh in the morning. She needs to rest."

Ashleigh felt a little better the next morning, when a steady stream of visitors stopped by the Griffen house—Charlie, Linda, Samantha and Mr. McLean, Clay Townsend, Hank, and some of the other stable staff. Ashleigh sat on the living room couch with her back supported by pillows, trying not to look as uncomfortable as she felt. She was sore from other bruises she'd acquired in the fall, and she couldn't turn her head without turning her whole upper body.

"It's not as bad as it looks," she told Mike, who had blanched when he saw the big brace around her neck. "I can start moving around more tomorrow."

"You should take it easy for a couple of days at least."

"I'm bored already," Ashleigh said. "How did Fleet Goddess look?" Since she couldn't go to the stable herself, she'd sent Mike up to give her a firsthand report.

"She looked fine. Sammy was with her, and Charlie and Hank were hanging around too.

Don't worry. She'll have plenty of baby-sitters."

"And Wonder and the colt?"

"They're fine too."

Ashleigh smiled, then frowned when she re-membered what her injury was going to mean to Fleet Goddess's training. She balled up her fist and pounded one of the couch cushions.

Samantha tried to stay calm as she faced her fa-ther in their small apartment. "Please, Dad! You've got to let me ride. You know I'm good. I'm sorry I went behind your back before, but Ashleigh really needs my help now," she cried. "There's no one else to ride Fleet Goddess so she can stay in train-ing. And she has a race coming up."

"One race isn't that important," her father said. "There'll be other races when Ashleigh's better."

"It's important to Ashleigh! The doctor said she won't be able to ride for at least a month, maybe more. There won't be any more local races after that. Please!" she begged.

Instead of answering her, her father grew silent. He went to the window and stared out into space.

"Mom would want me to do it," she finally said.

Her father started and turned to her with a jerk. The hurt expression on his face made Samantha want to crawl away, but she couldn't give in. She had to stand up for what she wanted.

"Your mother *died* exercising horses!" her father cried hoarsely. "Or have you forgotten?"

Samantha felt tears welling up and fought them

168

back. "Of course I haven't forgotten. I love Mom! I miss her! But she would *want* me to ride. We used to talk about it all the time, and if she's watching right now, I know she's saying yes. Why can't you at least give me a chance?" Samantha couldn't stand to see the pained look in her father's eyes a second longer. She jumped up and raced out of their apartment to the stable.

She fought to control her anger and disappointment as she went into Fleet Goddess's stall. She felt like throwing things, but she couldn't let her own horrible mood affect the filly. She put her arms around Fleet Goddess's silky neck. "Oh, Mom, if you're listening and watching, you've got to talk to him," she whispered. Then she buried her face in the filly's warm coat and let the tears trickle down her cheeks.

For the next couple of hours, Samantha sat in Fleet Goddess's stall, desperately trying to come up with a solution. When she heard footsteps coming toward the stall, she hunched down in a corner, trying to keep out of sight. She didn't want to see anyone or talk to anyone. But the footsteps stopped outside the stall, so she lifted her face, ready to glare at the intruder. It was her father.

"I need to talk to you," he said gently.

Samantha tightened her mouth stubbornly. "You don't have to look at me like that," he told her. "I've done a lot of thinking in the last couple of hours. I don't think I've been very fair to you since your mother died. I've been so wrapped up in

169

dealing with my own pain, I haven't given enough thought to *your* needs and feelings. All I could think about was that I couldn't bear to have anything happen to you, too. You're all I've got left."

Samantha felt herself softening. This wasn't what she'd expected.

"I was wrong to stop letting you do the things that are important to you," her father said, "just because I'm afraid of another accident. Charlie told me it was like taking a talented young Thoroughbred and never letting it out of its stall. One day it would kick the stall door down. Charlie was right, but I didn't listen to him then." He paused. "I just came from talking to Ashleigh, and she's reassured me that it's safe to let you ride Fleet Goddess, so it's all right with me if you still want to ride the filly. In fact, I'd like you to be able to help Ashleigh out. I've always known that you're a good rider."

Samantha was relieved and overjoyed . . . but near tears, too. She flung herself across the stall into her father's arms. He hugged her tight.

"I love you," he said.

"I love you, too, Dad."

16

BY THE END OF THE WEEK ASHLEIGH WAS WELL ENOUGH to go out and watch the morning workouts. Samantha had waited until Ashleigh could be there before taking the filly out on the oval. The change in Samantha since her father let her ride was incredible. She just seemed to glow. She had a definite rapport with Fleet Goddess, and Ashleigh was almost jealous to see how well the filly worked for Samantha as they galloped around the oval.

Mr. McLean came over to watch and stood with Charlie and Ashleigh. There was a touch of worry in his expression, but as Samantha and Fleet Goddess galloped past in fluid and majestic motion, a proud smile flickered on his lips.

"They work well together, don't they?" he said to Ashleigh.

"Yes, they do."

"I'll worry every time I see her in the saddle," he

added quietly, "but it's time for me to let her grow up. And your filly will definitely be ready for her race now."

Ashleigh had already arranged for Jilly to ride Fleet Goddess in the Keeneland race. Jilly had been glad to help her out, but Ashleigh felt the sharp disappointment of not being able to ride herself. She hated being inactive. She hated the constricting brace on her neck, and she'd probably have to wear it for at least another month.

The brace certainly got her a lot of attention when she went into school the next Monday. She'd missed the first week, and she still couldn't drive, so Linda offered to pick her up and take her to school.

As soon as the two girls walked into the school building, Corey and Jennifer hurried over.

"My gosh, look at you!" Jennifer cried.

"You sure did a number on yourself," Corey added. "Does it hurt?"

"No, it's just a pain in the neck." Ashleigh laughed at her joke. "I can probably go down to a smaller brace by next week. How were your summers? I haven't talked to you in ages."

"You know that Jennifer came with us to our place on Cape Cod, right?" Corey said. "We had a ball and met the neatest guys."

"What about Tony?" Ashleigh teased Jennifer. Jennifer had seemed pretty hot on the football star at the beginning of summer, though that didn't necessarily mean anything. Jennifer always had a waiting list of guys anxious to go out with her.

"Oh, he was there some of the time," Jennifer said, grinning. "He lives right outside Boston. And now he's back in Lexington."

"So you'll be seeing a lot of him."

"You bet I will."

"Hey, Ash," Corey said. "What's this about your moving?"

Ashleigh gave Corey and Jennifer the details and described the new farm. "I don't have to change schools or anything, though."

They talked until the warning bell rang. "You're in my homeroom," Corey told Ashleigh. "I told Mr. Cobb what happened to you. Let's see the rest of your schedule." Ashleigh pulled her schedule from her notebook, and the four girls compared classes. "Good," Corey added, "we're in physics together, and you and Linda both have Steiner for English. We'd better get going or we'll be late."

"See you at lunch," Linda called as she and Jennifer headed off down the hall. "I'll save you guys seats."

The following week the Griffens started packing for their move. Ashleigh fought back tears as she boxed up her memorabilia and treasures of the last four and a half years. She slowly turned the pages of her scrapbook, her eyes scanning the many clippings about Wonder's triumphs. There were photos of Wonder as a foal, a yearling, and a two-year-old. There were others taken in the winner's circle—

Jilly proud in the saddle, Wonder with her head high, and Ashleigh glowing as she held the reins. Then there were the photos of Ashleigh in the saddle at the Breeder's Cup, the most exciting day of Ashleigh's life.

Ashleigh felt her throat tighten. She put the scrapbook and photo album carefully into the packing box, rose, and hurried from the bedroom. So much would be changing! Her life just wasn't going to be the same. She went straight out to the paddock where the mares and foals were grazing. In another couple of weeks the foals would be weaned, but for now they frolicked with their dams and tore around the pasture, playing with each other.

Ashleigh whistled when she reached the paddock rail, and Wonder instantly lifted her head and trotted across the grass. She nuzzled Ashleigh fondly and gave a soft, loving whicker. Ashleigh felt the tears start sliding down her cheeks. She couldn't hold them back any longer. Wonder's Pride scampered up a moment later, stuck his nose over the rail, and gave a shrill whinny. Ashleigh quickly scratched his ears, but inside she was aching.

"I'm going to miss you both so much!" She bit her lip and choked back a sob. "I won't be living across the drive anymore. Someone else will be there, and I don't even know what they're going to be like. I don't know how they're going to treat you. If only you could come with us."

Wonder whickered again, sensing Ashleigh's

sadness. She rubbed her soft muzzle against Ashleigh's arm.

"Oh, girl!" Ashleigh threw her arms around Wonder's neck and buried her face in the mare's long, silky mane. Wonder waited patiently, but Wonder's Pride, not understanding what was going on, stuck his head between the top rails of the paddock and nudged Ashleigh sharply in the ribs.

Through misty eyes, Ashleigh looked over at him. He had his head cocked comically to one side, and he was studying her. "I'm being a big baby, aren't I?" she asked him. "It's not the end of the world, is it? I met the new breeding managers today. They're young, and they know horses. They seemed pretty nice and told me to come see you both whenever I wanted . . ." Ashleigh blinked back a new wave of tears. ". . . but it's not going to be the same . . ."

Wonder touched her soft muzzle to Ashleigh's cheek. "Yes, I love you, too, girl."

Mr. Townsend threw a small party for the Griffens the night before the moving van came to pack up their furniture. All the staff gathered in the training yard, where long tables of food and drink had been set up. Mike and Linda both came, and Caroline came home from college and brought Justin. Jilly was there and Craig Avery, Samantha and her father, and of course, Charlie, Ken Maddock, and all the breeding and training grooms and exercise riders.

After everyone had had their fill of food and drink, Clay Townsend stood on one of the benches and called for everyone's attention. "As you all know, we're going to lose some very special people. We're going to miss them, but at the same time we want to wish them well in their new endeavor!"

A cheer went up from the crowd. "We have a little something for you," Mr. Townsend added, "a token of our appreciation and good wishes."

Hank handed him a long, gaily wrapped package with a card taped to the front of it. He gave it to Mr. Griffen. "Congratulations and thanks from all of us."

Ashleigh saw that her father's and mother's eyes were misty. They hadn't expected this outpouring of affection. Mrs. Griffen took the card and opened it. Ashleigh, Caroline, and Rory looked over her shoulder. The card, wishing them well in their new home, was signed by everyone, and many had written a personal note. Ashleigh felt her throat tighten as her mother tore off the wrapping. Inside was a beautifully hand-carved and -painted sign that said GRIFFEN BREEDING FARM.

"Oh," Mr. and Mrs. Griffen said in one breath. "Thank you—thank you all so very much. It's lovely!" Mr. Griffen held up the sign for all to see.

Clay Townsend smiled. "It's the least we could do. Much luck to you."

Everyone started talking at once and crowding around the Griffens.

"Everybody's so *nice*," Ashleigh said tearfully.

"What did you expect?" Mike said, grinning. "Come on, let's go talk to Jilly and Craig. You and Jilly probably have some race strategy to work out."

Ashleigh was holding Mike's hand as they sat in the movie theater on Wednesday night. Her eyes felt so heavy, she could hardly keep them open. The next thing she knew, Mike was gently shaking her. "Movie's over," he whispered.

Ashleigh jerked awake. "It is?" she said groggily. "I'm sorry . . . I didn't mean to fall asleep."

"You probably needed it, the way you've been running around this week."

Ashleigh nodded. She'd been up at three thirty every morning to make the half-hour drive to Townsend Acres, to watch and call out instructions as Samantha worked Fleet Goddess. Then, after every workout, Ashleigh would carefully check the filly over, and she and Samantha would share the tasks of cooling, bathing, grooming, and bandaging the filly's legs. Then Ashleigh would change into her school clothes in the McLeans' apartment, and she and Samantha would drive into Lexington for school. In the afternoons Ashleigh would go back to the farm for a while to check on Fleet Goddess and visit with Wonder and Wonder's Pride. By the time she got home, she was exhausted, but she still had to help with the unpacking and get her homework done before bed at nine thirty.

"Why don't you leave it to Charlie tomorrow morning?" Mike said as they got into his pickup for the drive home. "You're not going to work the filly, since you're vanning her to the track in the afternoon."

Ashleigh shook her head stubbornly. "Charlie's taught me just about everything I know. But I've got to carry it through to the end. It's important to me."

Mike gave her hand a squeeze. "Yeah. I understand. I'd feel the same way."

17

"WE STILL HAVE A COUPLE OF HOURS TO GO," ASHLEIGH said to Samantha as they stood outside Fleet Goddess's stall at Keeneland. Ashleigh slid a finger under her neck brace and scratched an itch. She was in a smaller brace and she could move more freely, but wearing it all the time irritated her skin. "Let's take her out for a walk. She looks like she's getting a little antsy. The excitement's getting to her."

The filly had her head over the stall barricade, snorting as trainers, grooms, and horses passed.

Samantha grabbed the lead shank and went into the stall to bring the sheeted filly out. Her nearly black coat shimmered in the light as she flexed her powerful muscles.

"It's quieter up at the end of the shed row," Samantha said. Her freckled face looked a little pinched from growing nervousness.

"Let's head up there, then," Ashleigh said as she

smoothed a hand down the filly's neck. Fleet Goddess tossed her head and pranced. "Nice and easy, girl. You don't need to get excited yet. We'll just go out for a little walk, and you can see what's going on."

"Are you getting nervous?" Samantha asked as they walked along past the stalls.

"Do you have to ask? My stomach's jumping around like crazy. The field's much better than I expected. All the other fillies have more experience than she does, and two of them have won stakes races." The race Ashleigh had chosen was a nongraded stakes race at a mile, and Ashleigh was beginning to wonder if she had been too ambitious. Maybe it would have been better to put Fleet Goddess in another allowance race, which wouldn't have drawn such a competitive field.

"She would have won the last time if she'd seen that other horse," Samantha said quickly. "And she's not waiting on horses like she used to. She's much more on her toes now."

"Yeah, but I wonder if I'm asking too much of her," Ashleigh said worriedly. "*Every* other horse in the field has more experience, and we're asking her to go two furlongs longer than she did last time out." Ashleigh knew even as she spoke that she was overtired and because of it, the smallest worry seemed larger than life. But her eyelids felt like they had sandpaper behind them. She'd been too wound up to sleep well the night before.

"She likes the longer distance," Samantha said. "When you rode her in the last race, you said she still had plenty left at the wire. And she sure felt like that when I rode her. They've really got long odds on her, though. I'm surprised."

"I'm not," Ashleigh told her. "She's only raced once. And look at the competition she's up against today. A couple of these horses have incredible bloodlines—Danzig, Alydame, Devil's Bag. One of them's out of a mare by Secretariat."

"Charlie says people are starting to pay attention to her bloodlines since Son of Battle came in second in the Travers."

"Charlie said that, eh?" Ashleigh chuckled. "By the way, Sammy, I can't thank you enough for the help you've given me. I don't know what I would have done without you."

Samantha flushed at the praise. "But I wanted to help. I've been so happy riding."

"You've done a good job . . . a fantastic job. I'm almost jealous of how well you and Goddess get along."

"You shouldn't be."

Ashleigh smiled. "Well, I think it's great. You're good for each other. And Jilly knows how to get the best effort out of her."

"You wish you were riding, though, don't you?"

Ashleigh heaved a sigh. "I sure do. But there'll be other races. My neck won't be in this stupid brace forever."

When they returned to Fleet Goddess's stall, Mike, Charlie, and Jilly were all there.

"Hoped you'd taken her out for a little stroll,"

Charlie said, pushing back his hat. "How's she doing?"

"She's a little more relaxed now."

Jilly went to the filly and stroked her head. "We're going to go out there and knock them dead, right, girl?"

Fleet Goddess snorted.

Jilly laughed. "Hey, Ash, I heard one of the *Racing Form* reporters asking questions about her."

Ashleigh felt a little tremor in her stomach. "They haven't talked to me."

"Maybe not, but they sure know who you are, and they've dug up the stories about her sire." Jilly threw a look over at Charlie. "You wouldn't have anything to do with the reporters staying away from Ashleigh, would you?"

"I might have put a word in a few ears. After the race is plenty of time for talk. I'm going up to watch the next couple of races—see how the track's playing. Coming, Mike?"

"Sure," Mike answered. "Why don't you come, too, Ash? It'll do you good to get away."

"Yeah, and I'd like to see how the track is." Knowing that reporters had started asking questions made Ashleigh feel like she had even more on the line.

"I'll stay with Goddess," Samantha promised. "I won't be leaving the stall anyway, since my father's going to come looking for me later on. He came up this morning. He's got a horse in the first race."

"We won't be too long," Ashleigh said, "since

she's running in the sixth race."

Watching a couple of races did help take Ashleigh's mind off her worries. The track seemed to be favoring front-runners. It was fast along the rail—which was fine, since Fleet Goddess liked to run close to the lead. If Jilly could keep the filly near the rail just behind the speed horses, she could angle out, or go through an opening when they got to the stretch. Ashleigh had studied the charts of every horse in the field. Only one horse had a record of being a consistent front-runner, and she was known to burn up the early fractions. Ashleigh didn't want Fleet Goddess to get in an early speed duel and burn herself out, so she would have to tell Jilly . . .

Suddenly she dropped her head in her hands and sighed. There were so many things to think of. What was she going to tell Jilly?

Mike put an arm around her shoulders. "Try not to worry so much," he whispered. "I know exactly how you feel—I feel it every time Jazzman or Indigo races—but you've got to have some faith in the horse, too."

"I have faith in Fleet Goddess," Ashleigh said, lifting her head.

"Jilly knows what she's doing. And, Ash," he added, squeezing her shoulders, "it's not the end of the world if she doesn't win. She's young. She's learning, and she's up against a darned competitive field. If she can hold on to second or third, no one's going to sneer."

Ashleigh didn't say anything for a moment. She

was angry at Mike's last words: "If she can hold on to second or third." He didn't believe in Fleet Goddess's abilities. He thought she was over-matched. She shrugged his arm off her shoulders. "I'm going back to the barn."

"And they're in the gate," the track announcer's voice called. Ashleigh had her binoculars focused on the number-four post position, from where Fleet Goddess would break. Jilly sat ready in Ashleigh's maroon and silver silks. Fleet Goddess seemed to be standing calmly, but the horse beside her wasn't. It fidgeted for seemingly everlasting seconds before the attendant and jockey managed to calm it. Then the gate doors flew open.

Fleet Goddess broke in a rush. She was three strides ahead of the rest of the field as Jilly started angling her toward the rail. But they didn't want the filly in first—not yet. Jilly kept Fleet Goddess on a tight hold and let three horses pass. The number-one horse, who was known to be a speedball, took the lead. The seven horse went after her, and the three horse was outside of them and a half length back. Jilly had Fleet Goddess on the rail another half length behind, but Ashleigh could see that the filly wasn't giving Jilly an easy time of it. She was getting rank and trying to throw up her head.

Ashleigh groaned. "She's not settling," she said tightly. The five horse moved up outside of her. The field was tightly bunched for the first quarter mile, eight lengths covering all of them. Fleet Goddess and Jilly were closed in on the rail, and the filly still wasn't settling. Her neck was arched against Jilly's hold on her reins, and her strides were like lunges as she fought to get ahead. At least with Fleet Goddess on the inside, Ashleigh had a clear view as the horses pounded down the backstretch.

The race wasn't playing out even close to what Ashleigh had imagined. Her main worry had been to keep Fleet Goddess going once she got the lead. At this point there was no chance of the filly ever *getting* the lead. She was totally boxed in. Jilly couldn't even drop back and go to the outside unless she wanted to go around a five-wide wall of horses. Ashleigh willed herself, Jilly, and Fleet Goddess to have patience. A lot could still happen. Samantha was clinging to the seating rail in front of her. Charlie had taken his hat off his head and was wringing it in his hands. Mike had his jaw clenched so hard, the muscles stood out in his cheek. Even as Ashleigh watched him, she saw him look quickly over her way. Behind her was Mr. McLean, with his hands resting on his daughter's shoulders, but Ashleigh couldn't see his face.

"They're into the far turn. No one giving ground here!" the announcer cried. "A very tight pack! Rose d'Or has her nose in front. Chelsea Street is challenging. In behind, it's Danzig's Dream, Chocolate Ice, Alydame, and Fleet Goddess on the rail looking for room. . . ."

Ashleigh could see the filly's frustration. Fleet Goddess looked ready to run up the heels of the horses in front of her. The field churned out of the far turn into the stretch. The two speed horses stayed neck and neck.

"They can't hold on much longer!" Samantha cried. "One of them's got to tire!"

Ashleigh could barely breathe. Her stomach was all knotted up. "Give her room!" she growled through gritted teeth. Only two furlongs to go. Fleet Goddess and Jilly would never get through in time. The one and the seven horse were still locked in battle, but they were losing ground, Ashleigh saw. Another horse had taken the lead outside of them—and Fleet Goddess was still blocked in on the rail behind them.

"I shouldn't have told Jilly to save ground!" she cried to herself. She hadn't realized she'd spoken aloud until Charlie called back, "Couldn't do anything else!"

The announcer's voice was growing more excited as the field drove close to the wire. "Chocolate Ice and Alydame have moved up along the outside and have taken the lead . . . and they're moving away. Danzig's Dream and Rose d'Or, still in battle, are dropping back. Fleet Goddess is looking for room but has no place to go. She's boxed in.

"Alydame, Chocolate Ice, neck and neck, nose and nose . . . three lengths back to the rest of the field. This is turning into a two-horse race—but here comes Fleet Goddess! She's found an opening along the rail. Jilly Gordon has this filly moving.

She's making up incredible ground. Alydame is trying to hold on, but as they reach the sixteenth pole, Fleet Goddess is eating up the distance. Alydame is tiring and drifting out. Fleet Goddess has a clear shot through, and she's taking it!"

Ashleigh screamed at the top of her lungs, "Come on, Goddess! Come on, girl! You can do it!" The others were screaming around her. She heard Samantha's voice. "You can do it."

Now that she had an opening, Fleet Goddess roared through it.

"A few strides from the wire," the announcer cried, "and Fleet Goddess has the lead—and is lengthening it! It's Fleet Goddess—winning it by two lengths and going away! Then Alydame and Chocolate Ice. The others are far back."

Ashleigh let out a whoop of joy. She hugged Samantha, then Mike, then Mr. McLean. As usual, Charlie kept his emotions more in check, but his blue eyes were twinkling and his hat was still crushed in his hands. Seconds later they all trooped down to the winner's circle.

Ashleigh was trembling with happiness as the winner's photograph was taken and she heard the calls of congratulations from the crowd. Fleet Goddess had made some lucky bettors happy, coming in at thirty-to-one odds, though Ashleigh didn't think the odds would be that high the next time out. Ashleigh knew for sure there would be a next time, and maybe then, she would be in the saddle.

This is my filly, she thought as she looked

proudly up at the beautiful animal. *I picked her out and I trained her—and we won!*

She looked over at Samantha and saw the younger girl's face glowing. Ashleigh wondered if this was the same girl who had threatened to run away just a month before. Samantha had the filly's dark head in her arms and was crooning her praises. Fleet Goddess nuzzled her gently in return.

"If it wasn't for your help, Sammy, Goddess would never have been ready for this race," Ashleigh said softly. "Thanks."

"This is what I've always wanted," Samantha said, beaming. "I've never been so happy. I can't wait for her next race. I know she's going to be a champion, and in another year Wonder's Pride will start training."

"We're going to knock them dead, aren't we?" Ashleigh said, smiling.

"Yes, we are!" Samantha grinned from ear to ear.